MW01244822

Maroon:
An Enemy's Journey

Book 1

By Grace Tasker

ISBN: 979-8-9882684-0-6

Cover Design: Indra Renovstyawan
Editor: Kristin Campbell
Maplewood Map and illustrations: Grace Tasker

Dedication

This book is dedicated to my parents. I am thankful for their love and support. I would also like to thank my best friend for her inspiration and encouragement.

MAPLEWOOD

Stream

Great Oak

Maroon's Log

Violet's Den

Mahogany's Ledge

Aqua and Bronze's Burrow

Mahogany's Den →

The Open Clearing

Slate's Burrow

← Magenta's Den

Coyote Territory

Chapter One
Returning Home

Afox was resting in the shade of a tree. The wind blew by Maplewood forest. This fox was called Maroon, and she had a beautiful orange fur coat, so bright it sparked from her fur. She also had black paws and a black nose. Her muzzle was patched with white, and her neck down to her chest. The tips of her ears were black, and the inside had tufts of white fur. Her tail was black at the end, and below that was a big patch of white, followed by a black stripe. The rest of the way down was orange.

Maroon lived alone in a log, wrapped in a blanket of moss by a stream. The entrance to Maroon's log was small, perfect for her, and too small for anything larger than a fox. Though Maroon lived alone in her territory, she had neighbors—all foxes. Some lived in tunnels, and some lived in mossy hollows. They were all different, but they were all her friends. All except for one, and she hated that one, too. But each

one of those friends lived alone, as well. Foxes didn't usually live together, so it was always strange for Maroon to have her friends do stuff for her, such as give her food or help each other hunt.

Why should I have to rely on my friends when foxes depend on themselves? Maroon thought. But she enjoyed her friends and would always stay with them, no matter what happened.

Stretching up onto her legs, Maroon breathed in the fresh air, licked her nose, sighed, and then began to walk home. Her paws ached a little. She felt like she had been traveling all day. Luckily, she was almost home. Then she could go into her log and rest.

As the trees thickened and the forest changed, Maroon knew she was almost home. The territory marks of her friends told her that she had entered her homeland.

Passing by her neighboring friends' burrows, she knew her log was up ahead. Yelping with joy, Maroon trotted through the woods and toward her home.

As Maroon reached the entrance to her log, she heard a familiar bark. She turned to see a fox trotting toward her. This fox was almost all black, but there were some patches of orange mixed in with her fur.

"Violet!" Maroon recognized this beautiful, friendly fox as one of her friends.

Violet trotted over to Maroon and gave her a happy lick. "Maroon, I just needed to tell you about Slate," Violet said.

Maroon grumbled. Slate was one of Maroon's worst enemies. He was a blue-gray fox with caramel-colored legs and paws. Maroon remembered when he tricked everyone into thinking that a wolf was invading the territory. Then, when every fox looked around in terror, Slate laughed.

"You know I can't trust Slate!" Maroon growled.

"I know you dislike him, but I can't be against him. You know he's my friend, too," Violet replied kindly.

Maroon's fur fluffed up, but then she realized that Violet was only trying to be kind.

"Okay," Violet continued. "So, Slate has been sniffing up some strange smells, and he's worried about it becoming a threat and invading everyone's homes."

Maroon grumbled, "I think Slate just told you to tell me because he knows I can't trust a word he says."

Violet knew this could go on forever, so she just calmly replied, "Maroon, you can't just ignore Slate all the time. He could be telling the truth, and you won't listen to him. Then something bad could happen to you." Then, with a flick of her tail, Violet disappeared into the brambles.

***

After Maroon awoke from her nap, she yawned and stretched. She then looked up to see a draft of sunlight seeping into the cracks of her den.

Maroon padded to the edge of her stream and lapped up some water. While she drank, she spotted a fish dart right in front of her nose. Then she saw a mushroom just inches away from her. She trotted across the clearing and gobbled it up in one bite.

She thought for a moment about what Violet had said. Was she telling the truth about Slate sniffing up some strange smells? Maybe an animal that could invade her territory and some other neighboring foxes? She pushed that out of her mind and focused on an animal slowly walking toward her.

Maroon studied the animal and growled. She didn't like strange animals coming toward her without knowing what they were.

"Maroon, it's just me!" the creature said in fear.

Maroon studied the animal again and realized that it was one of Aqua's pups.

"Teal!" Maroon barked in surprise. "I didn't know it was you. You've grown so big over the past few days while I've been gone."

"I know!" Teal squealed in happiness. "How far did you go on your trip?"

"Well, far enough that I got to see the mountains."

"Really?" Teal squeaked excitedly. "I want to go on a three-day trip like you did!"

"Well," Maroon replied, "you'll have to wait—you are too young. But don't worry; in a couple of weeks, you will be as big and strong as all the foxes in these woods."

"I can't wait. I am so excited!" Teal shouted then ran off to tell his mom and siblings the news.

Meanwhile, Maroon was about to slip back inside her den when she saw something out of the corner of her eye. She turned and saw a rabbit. Then she quickly ducked back into a bush and spied on it.

Food! she thought.

The rabbit, unaware that a fox was close by, crept closer and closer to Maroon. Suddenly, Maroon launched herself from the bush and at the rabbit. The rabbit squeaked in terror, spun around, and hopped away. Maroon was close on its tail.

She opened her mouth, ready to spring and catch the rabbit, when something slammed against her side really hard, knocking her off her paws. It took a moment before she regained consciousness, and when she did, she looked up in surprise to see a coyote.

The coyote growled at Maroon and paced in front of her, ignoring the rabbit that had escaped.

"What is the meaning of this?" Maroon barked. "You let the rabbit escape. And why are you still here?"

"Well," the coyote replied, "you were chasing that rabbit on *my* territory!"

"I was not!" Maroon growled at him.

"Oh really? Why don't you take a look!" the coyote snarled.

Maroon glanced around and saw that she was indeed on the rolling hills of coyote territory. She could only see the trees of Maplewood in the distance.

"Well," Maroon said, "I must have been too distracted chasing that rabbit that I didn't notice that I had run into your territory."

"Foxes," the coyote muttered. "They have no sense these days, and they always make up useless excuses to get themselves out of trouble."

4

Maroon lowered her head. She just wanted to get away from here and go back home.

Then the coyote stopped suddenly, sniffed the air, and froze.

Chapter Two
The Plan

W hat's going on?" Maroon questioned, standing in fear, her fur bristling.

The coyote, with fear in his eyes, glared at Maroon. "Don't you know?" he questioned.

"No," Maroon answered. "I have no idea what's going on."

The coyote replied, "The bears, they are attacking the territory by the stream."

That's my territory! Maroon thought. *All my friends are there!*

"I have to go there now!" Maroon began to run.

"No!" The coyote cut in front of her. "Only go back there if you want to die!"

"But all of my friends are there. I have to help them!" Maroon tried to get around the coyote, but he just pushed her back and growled.

"You can't go back! There are more bears than you think. You need a plan first … Come," he spoke.

Maroon thought for a moment, *What if he's lying, and he just takes me farther away from my friends and hurts or kills me? But what if he is actually trying to help? I can't just leave my friends with no help!*

She looked at the coyote who was waiting for her to make up her mind. He seemed like he really was going to help her, so she followed him to what she hoped would lead her to rescuing her friends.

Maroon trekked on through the underbrush, keeping low to the ground. She could now hear sounds coming from the territory.

Unfortunately, the sounds were the growls of angry bears and the shrieking of foxes.

Maroon glanced back ahead of her. The coyote, who was still trotting onward, was going to help her … or so she hoped.

"Stop," the coyote called back. "We are nearing your territory, but we need a plan first, and I think I have the perfect one." Then he snarled, glancing at her.

Maroon backed away. *What's his plan? Why is he staring at me like that? Does his plan have something to do with me?*

"You!" The coyote stepped forward. "I want you to sneak back to your territory, stay behind the bears. Then, while they're distracted by your friends, you attack them from behind. That's when *I* come in."

Maroon was unsure. *Will that work?* she thought. *What if that makes things worse, not just for me but all my friends?*

Maroon shook her head. "It's too risky. I'm sorry, but I can't do that."

The coyote sighed and turned away.

Did she upset him? Well, she couldn't risk her life just to do what he wanted her to do.

"Well," she told him, "if you're not going to help me, then I will help myself and my friends."

The coyote looked at her. "Without a plan?" he snarled. "Oh, that's right, foxes don't have plans, do they?"

Maroon stiffened. If he was just going to mock her instead of helping her, she had better things to do.

"Fine!" Maroon snapped. "I'm going to save my friends all by myself. I don't need your help." With that, she turned and scampered away, glancing back only to see the coyote staring at her with an expression on his face that was more than anger. In fact, it wasn't anger at all.

Maroon brushed against the underbrush, keeping out of sight as she slowly crept back to her territory. She longed to help her friends, even save them if she had to. She just couldn't stand that she had been away when the attack had happened.

I'm not going to let that coyote tell me what to do, Maroon thought to herself. *If he isn't going to let me save my friends when they need it most, then I am not going to let him tell me what to do.*

She stopped when she heard animals crashing through the forest.

"I must be close," she mumbled to herself. "Now, all I need to do is save my friends. The thing that coyote told me not to do."

Then she continued on toward the sounds of danger. She stopped atop of Mahogany's ledge and looked down at the scene. Aqua was dashing around in circles trying to confuse her opponent, a black bear. Once, the bear tried to swat his left claw at her as she ran in the other direction.

Meanwhile, Violet was facing off with a different bear. She was halfway in a fox hole trying to bite the black bear's nose as it was trying to bite her.

Foxes were scrambling about, trying to escape the danger. Still, everywhere they went, they only came nose to nose with a bear who painfully swatted them back into the ruckus.

"They're surrounded!" Maroon gasped in horror, watching more and more of her friends unable to get up after being swatted several times.

The bears roared with approval when a fox was sent fleeing back into danger, and yet the foxes could only yelp with pain and gasp in fear.

Maroon saw all her friends. Violet was still in a tunnel. Aqua refused to move as she lay on the ground, along with Mahogany and Magenta. Bronze was thrashing wildly as a bear pinned him down, smiling triumphantly.

Maroon saw no sign of Aqua and Bronze's pups. Instead, she felt a wave of sadness come over her, thinking they were dead.

Where was Slate?

Maroon would regret it, but she didn't care if Slate was killed.

"Feed him to the bears, for all I care!" she spoke.

After hearing Bronze's cry of pain, Maroon realized she needed to help. But what could one fox do against five bears? The answer came to her …

Nothing.

Yet, she *had* to help. Maybe she could jump on the bears from behind like the coyote had said. Of course, that wouldn't be worth the risk, or would it?

Maroon looked back at her friends, at how helpless they were, either lying unconscious or dead. And Bronze had utterly given up on escaping, lying limp, allowing the bear to quickly make its killing blow.

"No!" Maroon thought out loud. "It is worth the risk!"

She summoned up all her strength then pushed off the ledge above the bears, full of encouragement. Eyes locked on the one bear she was aiming for, she let herself fall into battle.

Chapter Three
The Bear Attack

Maroon felt fur brush against her paws as she landed on a black bear's back. She quickly dug her claws into the bear to keep her footing as she sank her teeth into its flesh.

The bear roared with pain and rose onto its strong back legs, trying to shake Maroon off. Maroon felt her legs give way underneath her and scrambled for footing but was left clinging to a bear with her jaws, her legs flailing in the air.

The bear came crashing back onto all fours with an terrifying roar. The bear's landing was enough to send Maroon flying head over heels into the air.

She yelped with fear as she landed hard on the bear's head but clawed desperately at the bear's face. The scratches Maroon had made were now welling with blood.

The bear shook her off and put a paw to his face in pain.

Taking the chance, Maroon jumped to her paws, claws scraping the earth. She then hurled herself at the bear, crashing into its side and snapping at its flank.

The bear turned and looked wide-eyed at a vicious-looking fox. Then the bear spun around and reeled away into the forest, roaring in shock as it went.

Maroon smiled with glee, knowing that only four bears remained.

She turned and ran toward the sounds of Bronze's cries.

Emerging from a bramble thicket, Maroon saw Bronze sprawled on the grass. A bear, smiling with satisfaction, raised a paw to deliver the final killing blow.

Letting out an angered bark, Maroon charged at the bear. The bear stopped mid-swing and turned on Maroon, roaring in rage.

Maroon snapped at the bear, but the bear swung its paw and smacked her aside. The blow sent Maroon flying a few feet away. She landed with the wind knocked out of her lungs and a searing pain in her shoulder from the bear's swat.

Maroon scrambled to her paws, gasping in pain as she heaved herself up. Then she turned toward the sound of an angry roar, followed by the sound of plants being trampled as an animal came crashing toward her. As soon as Maroon turned to look, she faced a giant, angry bear looming above her.

Horror-stricken, Maroon turned and ran just in time to avoid a bone-crushing bite. With no idea where she was going, Maroon zoomed over a bush, realizing that the bear she had chased off was smaller and weaker than the one chasing her now.

The loud, angry roars of her pursuer attracted another bear's attention. It stopped what it was doing and, with an aggressive grunt, it lumbered over and took a stand between two trees, blocking Maroon's path.

Having no choice but to go right, Maroon turned and ran through a bramble bush as fast as possible, thorns tearing her fur.

With two terrifying animals on her tail, Maroon realized that the only escape was behind her pursuers because the other two bears were surrounding the clearing ahead.

Maroon made a sharp left turn in the direction of her stream and her log. But, no sooner than she did, Maroon realized she had made a big mistake. She had to go through a wall of bramble bushes to get to her log, which would waste enough time for the bears to quickly catch up. In the middle of the wall was a big oak tree, its roots long and wide enough for her to climb.

As if a bolt of energy went through her, Maroon ran as fast as she could, dashing across the dense forest and nearing the oak. Once she reached it, she launched herself into the air, landing awkwardly on a twisted root.

As she tried to get a better footing, Maroon stole a glance over her shoulder, seeing the bears hurriedly running toward her.

As panic began to overpower her, she regained her stance upon the root then hauled herself onto a higher, sturdier branch.

Hearing the loud, startling roar of a bear directly behind her, Maroon shifted her back leg. Horror prickled over every hair as she felt herself begin to slip. Hearing the excited grunts of bears below, Maroon knew she had to do something fast.

If I fall, Maroon thought quickly, *the bears will be right below me. There will be no escape from the jaws of death then.*

Knowing she couldn't let the bears snatch her out of thin air, Maroon needed to get on the ground.

Just as she was about to fall, Maroon jumped, enjoying the shocked looks from the two bears below. She would have almost made a successful escape, too, if she hadn't been swatted out of the air by a monstrous bear paw.

The swat sent her flying, and she slammed hard into the oak. Fierce, agonizing pain caused her to let out a weak yelp. She put a paw to her head as if it would help, only to yank it away when she felt searing pain. She looked down at her paw and gasped when she saw her usually black fur was blood-red. Her head was bleeding!

Trembling on weak, shaky legs, Maroon tried to stand, only to collapse in violent coughing gasps.

Remembering the bears, Maroon looked around for them. She knew she was trapped by the oak tree, seeing them block off her only escape routes.

Maroon rested her head on her paws as the bears approached, her eyes glazed with sadness. The lump of sorrow in her throat was making it difficult to swallow. Finally, she closed her eyes and, for once, allowed death to take her.

Nothing stirred, nothing but the sound of vicious snapping. Though she could hear angry roars and the sounds of animals snapping and biting, Maroon couldn't feel it. She guessed she had died and could only hear the bears snapping at her. Only when she realized she could still smell did Maroon question if she was dead.

If I am dead, Maroon thought, *why can I still feel the pain in my head?*

It was then that Maroon snapped her eyes open. She wasn't dead! She was still lying by the oak! But the bears were still snapping.

Maroon looked toward them. Though her vision was blurry, she could make out the two bears. They seemed to be facing something. She strained her eyes and finally make out a dog-like shape in the middle of the bears. Its pelt looked somewhat gray, somewhat tan. Though her vision was letting her down, Maroon knew it was Slate.

I knew it! Maroon thought. *Slate is helping the bears! And now he's going to enjoy killing me!*

However, as Maroon waited for Slate to rip her to shreds, it never happened. But the snapping continued.

Closing then opening her eyes again, Maroon was relieved to see clearly this time. Gazing out, she realized that the dog-like animal she had thought was Slate, who was growling and snapping at the bears, was more of a dusty gray color, not blue-gray like Slate.

To Maroon's astonishment, she realized who it was. The coyote!

Maroon just lay there in shock, silent, admiring what played out before her. The coyote, who had promised to help her fight the bears, though Maroon hadn't liked his strategy and had left him, had still come to fight! Maroon didn't know whether to be angered or relieved. He was saving her life right now.

A bear swung out a paw, roaring with immense rage. The coyote dodged fast on his paws, raking the bear with painful scratches. Then he turned and ran back, doing the same to the other bear. Only after one bear's nose was dripping with blood did it retreat. The other bear, though covered in wounds, didn't give up, still swinging its paws with full strength.

Meanwhile, the coyote was tiring. Not much longer and he would be killed.

When the bear was in mid-swing, there was a loud *bang!* Then there was a flutter of wings as the nearby birds were scared away. Other than that, the forest fell silent.

Chapter Four
The Bang

Maroon had forgotten entirely about her injuries and was just as shocked as everyone else to hear such as sound quite as loud like that. But, of course, Maroon, nor any of the animals, knew what to do.

Still up in the air, the bear lowered its paw then grunted and jogged in the direction the sound had come from.

No sooner than it had, Maroon decided to follow. But first, she had to find out what that sound had been. So, gasping as she tried to stand, she hobbled over in the direction of the sound, stopping only when she felt fur brush her pelt.

"Here," a voice spoke. "Lean on me."

Looking up to see the coyote, his gentle gaze relaxed Maroon. Leaning against him allowed her to walk easily. She was actually surprised at how often the coyote spoke to her.

"Take all the time you need. No rush. Do you need to stop? Would you like to stop here and catch your breath? I'm sorry about all of this."

Never had Maroon thought the coyote would be this patient with her. The last time she had been with him, he'd been mean to her. *Yet he did really want to help me*, she remembered.

"I don't think investigating whatever made that sound is safe," the coyote said.

Still, full of curiosity, they followed the stream in the opposite direction of Maroon's log. Finally, they came closer to the direction of the sound.

It was then that Maroon said, "I don't think I know your name. I would like to know."

"My name's Thrash, thanks for asking. What's yours?" he replied.

"Maroon," she told him.

"Maroon," Thrash said, smiling. "That's a beautiful name."

Maroon felt her happiness fade as they stopped and saw three bears lined in a row, looking surprised at what they saw. Maroon and Thrash pushed through them to see what had happened. The bears paid no attention to them but continued staring ahead.

Looking on with the bears, making sure they were well hidden from the cause of the sound, a wave of horror prickled over Maroon.

A bear lay by the edge of Violet's territory and the start of Aqua's. The bear was not moving, and a glistening pool of blood was around it. Its eyes were glazed with death, and its jaws hung open, as if it had been about to roar before it was silenced forever. Next to the bear was a man holding a stick in his hands, smiling proudly at the dead bear.

As soon as the bears that were still alive saw their dead friend, they all turned and ran, letting out low roars, promising not to return.

"What did that person do that could possibly kill a huge bear like that?" Maroon gasped loud enough to worry Thrash.

"Quiet!" he snapped. "What happened to the bear could happen to you."

"But … what happened to the bear?" Maroon asked, keeping her voice low.

"It was all that stick," Thrash replied. When Maroon gave him a questioned look, he continued. "You see, that's a trapper. Trappers are very dangerous because they like to kill and sell animals. No one knows why, but if you go near a trapper that has a stick, you will die in a second. When humans hold sticks, they can force it to make a loud noise, and that noise is what kills things."

Maroon was shocked into silence. The only movement she made was a slight twitch of her ear. *How could someone be so cold-hearted that they would kill innocent animals?*

15

Thrash spoke again. "They also set steel traps, like jaws, hidden on the ground, that will painfully catch your paw and hold you till death comes to you."

Maroon couldn't speak. Death was so unfair.

Thrash looked at Maroon, his gaze intense, and his voice stern. "Promise me you will stay far away from the trappers, okay?"

Maroon reluctantly nodded, stopping short to think about what Thrash had said. *He really does want to keep me safe, but why does he care so much about me?*

Looking back to see the trapper dragging the bear away, Thrash said, "He probably won't be back soon."

"How do you know?" Maroon asked.

Thrash looked back at Maroon. "I haven't seen a trappers' house anywhere near here; it's probably really far away."

Maroon nodded in agreement then suddenly remembered the cause of this conversation.

"My friends!" she shouted. "I have to find out if they're all right!" She turned, heart racing, but Thrash stood in her way.

"Wait!" he spoke. "I'm coming with you."

As if she was still being chased by a snarling bear, Maroon ran as fast as she could to the open clearing where her friends lay. Gasping in shock, she saw the limp, furry bodies of her friends sprawled upon the floor.

Getting her senses back, Maroon rushed over to the nearest orange pelt. It was Mahogany. Her chest steadily rising and falling told Maroon she was alive—alive but unconscious.

Maroon leaned over and began licking. The quick, rhythmic strokes from her tongue caused Mahogany's breathing to quicken. She was waking up! Still, the fox would not budge. Maroon noticed how heavy Mahogany's eyelids were, so she began to carefully sweep her tongue over them. Feeling her eyelids flutter caused Maroon to back away, waiting with anticipation for Mahogany to stir.

First, there was a slight twitch of her ear. Then Mahogany opened one eye then the other. Maroon felt relief wash over her, so much so that it caused her to stumble into a sitting position.

Mahogany propped herself up, gasping. "Maroon, what happened to you? Your head … it's …" She stopped abruptly and winced. "What happened to me?"

Mahogany had a bruise above her right eye and a large red scratch on her shoulder.

"No time to explain. Help me with the rest of our friends!" Maroon snapped as she turned and was about to run to her other friends when she was face to face with Thrash. There was another fox behind him with equally bad scratches.

"Maroon," Thrash spoke, "I found another of your friends. This one says he goes by Bronze. He's lucky to be alive."

Maroon glanced at Bronze, happy to know he was safe, then replied, "Did you say another friend?"

"Yes, actually, I helped another red fox. She was too surprised to see a coyote that I didn't get her name, but she is alive, and she said she needed to get to her burrow to check on something," Thrash finished.

"Must be Aqua. Bronze, why don't you go with her to check on your pups?" Maroon asked.

Bronze nodded then fled in that direction.

Soon, Maroon and Thrash managed to wake up the last two foxes that had been knocked out by the bears. All of Maroon's friends were wounded but alive.

Not long after, Maroon heard paw steps behind her. She spun around and felt a growl rise in her throat. Slate had returned.

He stopped in his tracks when he saw all his friends, dropped his prey, and gasped.

17

Chapter Five
Slate Returns

W hat happened?" Slate, a blue-gray fox with caramel colored legs and a white chest, exclaimed, looking from fox to fox, open-mouthed at what he saw.

He had just returned with a freshly killed bird that he dropped from his jaws. His coat was still clean, not an injury in sight.

Maroon inched closer to Thrash, standing by his side, signaling that Slate was someone she wanted to avoid.

Thrash raised his lips in a snarl and stood defensively in front of Maroon.

"Who and what is that thing?" Slate asked.

"Slate!" Violet cried, breaking away from everyone and running toward him. She stopped right in front of him and began nuzzling him. Soon after, the rest of Maroon's friends ran up and did the same, relieved that Slate had returned. But Maroon was outraged.

Why are they happy to see him? she thought. *Don't they know he was the cause of all this? The reason the bears attacked, the reason everyone had to get hurt? No one would suddenly disappear right when we were ambushed unless he knew it would happen.* Those thoughts soon led up to others.

All of this is Slate's fault! When Violet said Slate was sniffing some strange smells, he must have been bringing the bears around to tell them where to attack. So, by saying he thought he smelled something, he seemed less suspicious. Then Slate disappeared because he knew the bears would attack. He planned it! And he decided to go hunting, so it looked like he was busy rather than just gone for some time.

Maroon was so angry that she sprung herself forward without warning. Shoving her friends aside, she let out an aggressive bark. "Traitor!" she spat.

Taken aback by the sudden snarl, Slate abruptly backed up. Then, tripping over his bushy tail, he stumbled and fell, cowering on his stomach.

"Wha-what-what did I do?" Slate mumbled, staring up at Maroon with a lowered head and his ears lying flat.

Annoyed by Slate's act of helplessness yet pleased she was spilling out the truth, Maroon said, "You know what you did."

Violet gasped and pushed Maroon aside. "Maroon! What are you doing?" she cried.

Maroon snarled, showing her teeth. Then she slowly lowered herself to sit. "I know what he did," she said proudly. "And just because all of you guys care about Slate and will defend him doesn't mean he's innocent."

Then she rose to all fours and said, "Come on, Thrash; let's go." With that, she and Thrash walked deeper into the woods, leaving her shocked friends and a traitor.

***

Maroon lay in her log, intently thinking. Thrash had left Maroon to herself and was over by the creek, tail flicking.

Maroon sighed and rested her head on her paws. *How don't they know?* she wondered. *If Slate left at the exact time the bears attacked, shouldn't it be obvious he knew it would happen? So, if he left to save himself, he didn't care what he left behind. He wanted us all to die. Or, he could have left to go tell the bears to attack. But instead, he was on their side! How could he do such a thing to all his friends! Even Violet is so nice to him, and he just tried to kill her! I hate Slate! I hate him!*

"Traitor!" Maroon shouted, standing on all fours, tail thrashing wildly. "Acting all innocent … Well, I know what he did, and it's not pleasant."

Then, seeing nothing better to do, she lay back down.

The moon rose, but she hadn't slept since the bears attacked. She had planned to go to sleep through the day but had never gotten the chance.

Great, now I'll sleep through most of the night, she thought, annoyed, knowing nighttime was safer due to its shadowy darkness. But she hadn't realized how hungry she was. *I'm too tired to hunt.* Maroon growled when she heard the desperate groan of her empty stomach. *The only food is that bird Slate brought back, but I'm not going to touch that Slate-infected creature.*

Heaving a heavy sigh, she slowly closed her eyes, relieved with the sudden peace she felt.

***

Where am I? was the only thing she could think as she glanced around. Everywhere she turned, everywhere she looked, she only saw an unnatural gray-blue fog that filled her nose with a horrid, acrid scent. The fog was so dense that she couldn't see where she went.

Then there were the sounds. The bone-chilling sounds were the screaming of foxes. Each sound of a fox she knew. Mahogany, Aqua, Magenta, Bronze, Violet! The echoing shrieks were silenced by a growl, a terrifying growl.

Blindly, she ran through the fog. On she stumbled until she crashed into an oak tree. So vast and tall, its naked branches reached the sky, seeming to haunt the acrid green atmosphere with its deadly spears.

Then she heard a shrill yelp, sending horror through her veins.

With her back turned to the oak, she faced the sound, but it seemed to come from every direction. Then she heard a roar and crashing of paws from an unknown animal.

Locating the approaching threat, she snarled, showing her teeth, claws digging into the dry, dead earth. All she could do was growl defensively as a shadow formed in the mist. Then, as it approached, she could see the slick, bony shape of a fox. She gasped as she looked up at Slate.

He cackled, sending a shiver down her spine, and he stared down at her. He seemed to double in size, and his cold, red eyes, along with his fangs revealing gleams, caused her hackles to rise with terror.

She tried to run but was blocked by the unliving twisted oak. Panicked, she looked back. No sooner than she did, jaws enclosed around her.

Laughing hideously, Slate swallowed her up.

Yelping, Maroon kicked, thrashing to get out of her enemy's jaws. Spraying up dust, she panted, realizing it had only been a dream. But it had seemed so real.

She knew what her dream meant. Slate was a traitor, and now he was going to pay.

Sitting up, Maroon peered out of her log. The moon was still high in the sky, telling her there were still many more hours to come before dawn. She stretched only to feel her hunger rise, adding discomfort to her belly.

Appearing from her log, Maroon felt peace. The moonlight shone on the water, crickets chirped, and there was an occasional scurry of those small animals awake at night. The forest was so peaceful at night. No wonder Maroon liked it better. During the daytime, it was unpleasantly loud—bears roaring as they chased her, the chatter of noisy animals, and everything seemed out to get you. But night brought peace, and Maroon needed it after her awful dream.

Maroon padded down to her stream, the grass cool beneath her paws. Bending down, she lapped up the moonlit creek. The cold water trickled down her throat as if soothing her, but it reminded her it was empty when it reached her stomach. Sighing, she looked out at the bushes, hoping her prey would show itself to her.

She started moving to her left, not seeing anything, keeping her senses alert. Reaching her oak tree, she sniffed at it, knowing lots of small animals loved the many hiding places the roots provided. Smelling the scent of a mouse but realizing it was stale, Maroon turned and began searching the surrounding wall of bramble bushes. She couldn't find anything there either.

Maybe hunting outside my territory is best, she thought, knowing that once she went through the surrounding bramble bushes, that was when she would be out of her territory. Her hunger told her to go.

She pushed herself through the bramble bushes, claws digging into the earth, not minding the thorns that brushed her fur. Once out, she began searching.

Ears pricked, nose to the ground, and paw steps as quiet as she could make them, she hunted. Finally, after what seemed like a long time, she picked up the scent of a crow. Following the smell, she stalked forward, lifting up her head to see if she could catch sight of the bird. Then, after passing a bush, she did catch sight of it. The black-feathered bird flapped about and cawed angrily as it chased something. Peering from behind the bush, Maroon noticed that something was moving and trying to get away from the crow.

So that's why the crow is awake at night. It is trying to murder this innocent creature. Maroon paused. *Speaking of trying to murder this innocent creature, I'd better put an end to this.*

Jumping from the bushes, Maroon snarled. The crow soon forgot about its furry snack and was up in a flutter of wings and caws. But Maroon was too fast. She pounced on the bird and killed it, clutching it between her teeth.

Relieved to finally have something to eat, she turned her attention to what the crow was after. It was small and cowering in fear with its long ears against its tiny head.

A baby rabbit! Maroon thought, pleased to see it alive. *And I saved it from this crow.* Knowing the rabbit was cornered, Maroon decided to make her move. *Now I can bring something back for Thrash*, she thought joyfully but stopped.

The baby bunny was just trapped there, pleading for its life. Ears down, paws on the ground, eyes big and sad, and a continuously twitching nose. Maroon noticed a tuft of fur on the top of its head. She sighed. *I can't kill this baby rabbit. It has hardly been on this earth, and what's the point in saving it if I'm just going to kill it?*

She picked up her crow and began to walk back home. Then, turning around, she looked into the deep black eyes of the rabbit. Knowing she was letting it live, it raised its head and its ears in curiosity. Maroon nodded, warning the rabbit, and then bounded back to her log.

After eating all her prey, Maroon made her way out of her log once more. Enjoying the moonlight, she trotted over to her stream to quench her thirst.

Approaching the water, she saw Thrash. Smiling, she sat down next to him, pelts brushing together.

Both looking down at the stream, Maroon spoke. "Thrash, I'm leaving."

Thrash's smile soon disappeared as he turned to look at her. "Leaving? Why? When?"

"I'm leaving tomorrow. I can't stay here knowing what Slate did. I don't feel safe here anymore." Maroon sighed.

"Look, I know you hate Slate, but—"

"You don't understand!" Maroon interrupted then explained her suspicion of Slate being a traitor.

Thrash nodded. "Well, now I know why you called him a traitor. Do your friends know?"

Maroon shook her head. "They don't know I'm leaving or about Slate. I just hope they stay safe from him." She looked at Thrash. "I'd like you to come with me but … my friends don't know the danger they're in."

Thrash licked Maroon's ear. "Don't worry; I'll stay here and make sure Slate doesn't do anything. Be safe … promise?"

Maroon nodded. "I promise. Are you sure you don't mind not coming?"

"I don't mind if seeing your friends safe makes you feel better," he said, smiling. "Will I ever see you again?"

Maroon sighed. "I don't know. If Slate isn't causing trouble, you can come and visit me."

Thrash agreed. Then, for the last moments they would spend together, the two friends sat side by side as the morning slowly came.

Chapter Six
Maroon Announces the News

As morning arrived, Maroon sat in her log, thinking of the best way to tell her friends the news about her leaving. *They would understand, right?* she thought to herself. *Why I think staying is dangerous. Or will they get mad at me?*

Maroon shook her fur. *If they get mad, maybe I shouldn't tell them my thoughts on Slate. They shouldn't get mad at me for leaving, anyway.* She opened her mouth with a big yawn.

Moments later, she heard the paw steps of someone approaching. She raised her head as Violet stuck her head into Maroon's log.

"Maroon," Violet began, "I'd like to talk about what happened yesterday."

Maroon sighed. "Why yesterday?"

Violet replied, "Because yesterday, you threatened Slate for no reason!"

"For no reason?" Maroon began. "For no reason! Oh, I'm trying to protect you! You think you know him, don't you? Well, trust me. He did something that only Thrash and I know about."

Violet snarled, "Maroon! What has gotten into you! Slate would do nothing harmful! He's the sweetest fox I've ever known. But, speaking of doing nothing harmful, what is it you think he did?"

Maroon flicked her ear in annoyance. "Isn't it obvious? He left when the bears attacked! He's the one that caused it! He's a traitor!"

Shocked, Violet said, "Maroon, he went *hunting* when the bears attacked. He told me."

"Exactly! He *told you* he was going hunting so you wouldn't follow him!" Maroon barked. "He wanted you to stay home so he could tell the bears to kill all of you!"

Violet looked angry. "Slate would never do that! Just because you hate him …"

"That's why I'm leaving …" Maroon mumbled, feeling like now was the right time to announce the news.

"What!" Violet gasped. "You can't leave. And all because you hate someone!"

"No, it's actually because I don't feel safe here knowing what Slate did."

"I don't care what you think Slate did!" Violet interrupted. "He didn't do anything that had to do with the bears! If you leave, you're not solving any of your problems."

"I'm keeping myself safe, and I suggest you do, too. But because I know you'll stay with Slate, I told Thrash to keep you safe," Maroon said.

Violet looked puzzled. "Who's Thrash?"

"The coyote," Maroon answered.

"The *what*?" Violet shouted, eyes blazing in anger. "You told that coyote to stay here with all of us!"

"To keep you safe. Especially from Slate," Maroon argued.

"Slate isn't going to do anything!" Violet exclaimed. "What about Aqua and Bronze's pups? Don't you think the coyote will eat them?"

"Please," Maroon said, sighing. "He has a name. But knowing Thrash, he wouldn't hurt anything."

Violet sighed. "Fine, he can stay, but you're going to have to tell everyone about your news because I'm too ashamed of you to do so myself."

Maroon stood up. "Well, at least we settled one thing—I'm leaving—but I wish you believed me about Slate."

Violet frowned. "Well, I'm not too pleased to be living with a smelly forest dog while you're out having the time of your life. Also, accusing Slate of something he didn't do."

Maroon twitched her tail. "Again, he has a name. Besides, foxes should be living on their own, anyway. I'm doing Slate a favor if I leave, and I hope you make the wise choice of getting away from him, as well."

Violet flattened her ears. "Whatever. Just come on and get this over with."

The walk with Violet seemed to take all morning. She wasn't hiding her anger at all but storming ahead, a glint of annoyance in her eyes and revealing her fangs in rage. Maroon couldn't walk comfortably beside her because anger and frustration were sparking from Violet's pelt like lightning.

Maroon saw Aqua and her pups as they reached the open clearing with Bronze and Magenta. Teal was bouncing around in the tall grass with his sisters, Taupe and Mauve. Mauve was a light-red-pelted fox pup, while Taupe had blonde-red fur. Teal was a playful pup with a rusty red coat.

Maroon watched as Teal jumped onto a rock, yapping in delight. Mauve and Taupe were chasing each other, circling around the stone.

As Maroon and Violet approached, Magenta stopped her conversation with Bronze and Aqua, turning to bark happily as Maroon stopped and sat.

"Maroon, how are you today?" Magenta asked, her tail carefully wrapped around her paws.

"Well …" Maroon began, "I'm doing—"

"She has something to tell you all," Violet interrupted in a snappy tone. "Now, you all just stay here while I gather everyone else." Violet turned and bounded away with a promising stare, leaving Maroon to frown.

Why does she always have to make a big fuss over everything? she thought. *When I say I'm leaving, she acts like it's the worst thing ever, and she gets so mad.* Maroon flattened her ears, annoyed by the thought.

"So, what do you need to tell us, Maroon?"

It was Aqua's voice that disturbed her.

27

Turning to face Aqua, Maroon felt her fur rising. "I, uh …" *How am I going to tell them?* Maroon paused to think. *Their pups love me around. Teal will be so sad.* She remembered all the fun times she'd had with him. For example, she taught him how to pounce on beetles, play tag, and have fun in her stream. *It will be upsetting to leave him,* she thought to herself. Then she reminded herself of the reason she had to go. *Slate! Oh, I hope Thrash will keep the pups safe!*

"Maroon?" Bronze's voice brought her back to her senses. "You were saying?"

"Oh! I just, um … well, I think we should wait until everyone else has gathered," she spoke, not too excited to tell the news.

The nods from her friends told her they understood.

Good, I don't want to have to tell them now, Maroon thought.

Hearing the chirping of birds, the trickle of her stream, and the wind whispering through the trees made Maroon think how lovely and calm the daytime was today. The warm rays shining on her back, the sweet nectar-scented air she breathed in, and the cool, soft grass under her paws.

But the thoughts were soon silenced by the padding of paws coming toward her. She could tell who they were by sound. Softer, lighter paw steps were the rest of her friends, including Slate by the extra paw steps. The significant, more giant paw steps were Thrash. The smaller but loudest paw steps were Violet, storming her way toward her.

Opening her eyes, Maroon saw Violet gathering her friends around and sitting them down. Once Violet was finished, Maroon was uncomfortable with all their eyes on her.

Maroon cleared her throat then spoke, "Well, as you all know, I need to tell you something important. Some of you may know already." She looked to Thrash, who nodded. "It sort of has something to do with me threatening Slate yesterday," she spoke, noticing Slate's eyes widen. "I just want you all to know," she continued, "I'm leaving.

"What?"

"No!"

"Leaving?"

"Why?"

Maroon heard the responses being thrown at her. She gathered her breath and shouted over the yelling, "It's to keep myself safe!"

"Safe?" Bronze spoke. "From what?"

"Slate," Maroon responded then began to tell everyone about Slate and the bears.

During the whole thing, Slate looked upset. He looked at Maroon with his ears down, shoulders slumped, and his eyes were like nothing Maroon had seen before. Maroon noticed her mouth was ajar and shut it, looking away from Slate.

You can't fool me, she kept to herself. *I know you're a traitor.*

Not allowing any more questions from her friends, Maroon approached them.

Mahogany smiled. "Maroon, I'll miss you. Safe travels." She nuzzled Maroon.

Maroon moved to Bronze, Aqua, and their pups.

"Do you have to go?" Teal asked, disappointed.

"Yes," Maroon replied, licking each pup then looking up at Bronze and Aqua. They seemed sad but still smiled. Maroon nuzzled them both. "Take care."

Then she turned to Slate and whispered in his ear, "If you so much as touch any of my friends, I will have my coyote friend here tear you apart!"

Slate closed his eyes and covered his face with his tail once Maroon said goodbye to Magenta.

She approached Violet. "Goodbye," she said and tried to nuzzle her, but a scowling Violet snapped at her.

"I don't want you near me!"

Maroon frowned, knowing Violet would regret that later.

She turned to Thrash, smiling, and stepped forward to lick his nose.

Grinning, he said, "Bye, Maroon. Thanks for all you did."

Maroon said goodbye once more then turned and walked away.

After she walked a couple paw steps, she heard Aqua say to Slate, "Don't worry, Slate. We don't think you did anything that Maroon said you did. You aren't a traitor."

That was followed by a chorus of barks in agreement from all her fox friends.

Maroon flattened her ears. *Thrash will keep them safe if they aren't wise enough to*. Then she trotted on.

Chapter Seven
A Journey's Start

Maroon had not gotten far from her territory when she felt a pang of emptiness. She was leaving her friends behind, so why shouldn't she feel bad?

No, she thought. *They chose to stay. I had to leave my friend with them. I'm making the right decision, and I shouldn't be sad about it.*

But why did it feel like she had left a piece of herself behind? Maroon started to think about her friends. She loved how Magenta would sometimes gather everyone around at night, and they all would have a small feast and chat, and the pups would play under the moon. That was something they had always enjoyed. Then Maroon remembered how Mahogany was always collecting things. She had gathered acorns, honeycombs, moss, and even shiny objects. Mahogany was always finding something new. She reminded herself about Aqua and Bronze and how they were such a perfect couple, always doing things for each other, no matter what, and their pups! Maroon just adored those pups like they were her own. They talked, laughed, played, and shared their feelings with her, causing Maroon to glow with happiness at the memory. She was going to miss those pups, especially Teal, who was the one who always knew how to cheer her up when she needed it or would remind her how to do things his way. She wished he were with her so he could tell her what he would do right now as she padded through the forest.

But I already decided what I wanted, or have I? Remembering how Violet snapped at her when she had left caused Maroon to break into more thoughts about her. Maroon always remembered how Violet would tell Maroon all about her problems. If Violet made a big mistake or needed help with something, or even if Violet made someone mad and needed to talk about it, Maroon was always beside her, comforting her no matter how upsetting Violet's problems would get.

Oh, Violet, she thought, *why couldn't you comfort my problem, as well? Why did we have to fight? Why did I have to leave you like this?*

Maroon turned to look back. All she could see was the thick mangrove of trees. She reflected back to how far she had traveled, yet how unaccomplished she felt. Maybe if she went further, she would start feeling better.

On she went, her paws crunching on leaves as she walked, the sunlight seeping into her pelt and warming her. The birds, always cheerful as they chirped, started to cheer her up, as if telling her she made the correct decision.

Maroon had covered a lot of ground while the sun rose to its highest peak. Shining brightly onto her back seemed to make her realize she was starting to become hungry again.

Maroon searched for food, keeping her nose to the ground and eyes alert. Having stepped on many dead leaves since she'd left, Maroon decided to tread softly this time, trying not to make any noise as she hunted.

Having moved on for quite a while, Maroon felt the breeze begin to change. The air had become relatively dry and the wind rather cold as it swept through her pelt. The sky was full of dreary gray clouds that covered the sun, keeping it from spreading its warm rays. Winter was on its way, and it was not far from coating the earth in its cold blanket of snow.

Maroon's paws grew sore as the evening slowly grew darker, telling her dusk was approaching. Maroon stopped to lay down and lick her sore pads, feeling the aching pain slowly becoming soothing comfort.

Suddenly, a sound stole her attention. Maroon jumped to her paws, ears alert and legs prepared to run. Swiveling her ears, she located where the sound had come from. She ducked behind a rock when she heard it again. It was a low sort of moan, but also like a growl. It echoed through the trees, sending a shiver up her spine. Maroon then heard a lot of snapping and biting from the teeth of an animal, many animals.

Then there was the loud howl of animals and moans from the animal she'd heard first. Maroon listened to the sound of an animal breaking into a run. Then, bursting from the trees came a moose, its eyes wide in fear and moaning loudly. It was a male with a massive body and big antlers. It seemed troubled as it ran, and Maroon could tell why.

After the moose ran out of the bushes, a pack of wolves burst out, growling, chasing, and snapping at the moose's legs. The wolves ran. Most had gray, black, tan, brown, or silver coats, but one, the largest and burliest, had a pure white coat, so beautiful and magnificent as they ran. Maroon watched from her rock. Then the white wolf, the wolf in the lead, stopped.

It must be the Alpha, Maroon thought as the other wolves raced on.

Horror pricked through her bones as she realized he must have noticed her. Maroon shrank behind the rock.

The white alpha wolf turned to look in her direction, his yellow eyes as cold as a frozen sun. Maroon felt fear escaping from her pelt.

The white wolf raised its nose and sniffed the air. Maroon's eyes widened.

Then the wolf growled, raising a paw then planting it on the ground like a cold stone. He raised another paw, jaws parted, teeth revealed, and every step caused Maroon to clench her teeth, unable to stop the trembling of her limbs.

A howl came from one of the wolves, "Alpha, where are youuu?"

The white wolf stopped, ears pricked, head turned toward the howl. He looked back to face Maroon's rock and growled, then turned around and ran.

The distant howls slowly faded away as the wolves grew farther and farther from her. Maroon sighed in relief. She let herself relax, licking her fur clean.

That was close, Maroon thought. *I'll need to be more careful. This forest doesn't welcome only foxes. If wolves live here, so could other animals.*

Maroon began to rise on all fours, afraid of running into another animal. She began to walk farther, relieved the chill under her fur was just the wind.

Maroon thought for a moment, *Those wolves were scary hunting that moose. But, wait! Don't moose like water and standing in ponds? Maybe if I retrace its steps, it will lead me to the water!*

Excitement surged through her as she bounded toward a thicket. Nose to the ground, she picked up the scent of moose and the musky smell of wolf. Taking in big whiffs of air, Maroon padded along, following the trail. Once or twice, she would step into a wolf's paw print, only to take her paw out in fear. She shivered, seeing how massive the wolves' paws were and how sharp their claws must be.

After she had walked a while, she found it. The pond! Maroon yelped in joy and ran to the water's edge, causing some bugs to stay clear of her. The water tasted cool and refreshing, quenching her thirst. She saw birds fluttering above the water, trying to drink before winter struck. The last of the water bugs flew lazily, as if their energy had been sucked out of them. The pond made sounds—insects chirping, birds tweeting, and frogs croaking before diving down to hibernate in the water.

Maroon sat and watched the sky. The birds danced in the air, and the dark, gloomy clouds covered the sun as it began to set. Maroon could feel the storms coming. They were almost here.

Rising onto all fours, Maroon's fur prickled as the wind's chill made her shiver. Maroon broke away from the pond and raced for the cover of trees. On she ran, dodging and swerving through trees and rocks. She continued to move until her paws ached like thorns stabbing into her. Then Maroon stopped, panting. Her chest felt like it was on fire, and her panting was no help.

Maroon had forgotten about her injuries from the bear attack. She turned and saw her shoulder had a big scratch across it—red and swollen. She had not reopened it—that was fortunate—but she needed to rest and treat her wounds. Then Maroon felt the cut that the oak had given her, putting a paw to her head. It wasn't swollen like her shoulder, but it definitely needed her to rest.

Sniffing the ground, Maroon tried to locate the nearest shelter. However, her nose would not sniff out what her eyes could see. Looking around, she saw trees and rocks but no empty logs. Maroon started padding along, ignoring the small animals that fled before her. She wanted shelter more than food, mainly because of the coming weather.

After walking over rocks and around shrubbery, Maroon caught sight of a pine tree with low-hanging branches covered in many pine needles. That seemed suitable for her.

She trotted over and began digging a small sleeping place under the tree. Scooting pinecones out of the way, Maroon lay down, sighing with relief. She had finally stopped moving, and now she could rest.

Wrapping her tail around her and tucking her nose underneath it, Maroon closed her eyes and fell asleep. As she slept, the clouds gathered and began releasing the snowflakes that told the forest that winter had come.

Chapter Eight
The Gem Necklace

The cold, dry air Maroon breathed was what woke her. Snapping open her yellow eyes, she yawned. Then she sat up and looked around.

The earth was covered in a soft blanket of snow. The snow and ice glistened in the rising sunlight, and the leafless trees were heavy as snow rested upon their branches. It was such a beautiful day, and Maroon did something she hadn't done ever since she'd left. She smiled.

Rising onto her paws, she stretched then shook herself from head to tail, flinging off the dust from her fur. Then, sticking her head out, she leaped into the air, landing squarely on her paws as the snow crunched underneath her. She cocked her head and lifted up a paw before placing it back down, enjoying the returning crunch of snow.

She had seen snow before many times, but it was always a wonder how a season of fun could just fall out of the sky.

Jumping up into the air again, she felt a soothing coldness as she stuffed her face into the white substance. Yelping with delight, she bounded through the snow, kicking up chunks of it. Every hair on her body tingled with joy as Maroon jumped, ran, and rolled in the snow. It was her own fun time out in the middle of nowhere.

Unexpectedly, there was a small crash as a pinecone fell from a tree, but it was enough to startle Maroon back to her senses. She jumped and scrambled away.

"I shouldn't let myself get distracted like that," she told herself as she ran. "Being alone with no one to watch my back is dangerous, especially with some animals I've already seen somewhere."

As her hunger rose, she slowed her running to a trot. Panting, she sniffed the air. Vapor billowed out of her nose in the cold.

Taking a step forward, she looked around. Trees and gorse thickets surrounded her. To her left was a rock cliff. It was so big and tall, with moss on every boulder, darkened by shadows. It almost looked like an abandoned human structure. Maroon could not see how long it was, but she noticed a cave in the rock wall.

Forgetting about hunting and letting her curiosity pull her forward, she approached the cave. Her paws hardly made a sound as she treaded lightly on the soft snow. Anticipation gripped her as she steadily approached the dark cave. Holding her breath, she pushed through the unwelcoming wall of blackness.

Passing the smooth rocky entrance, she looked around. Her eyes adjusted, and she could almost clearly see the surrounding wall of moss that aligned the rocks around her. The cold air whispered in her ear, calling her. She looked in one direction, confirming that was where it had come from. Then, leading herself forward, her paws tickled on the gravel protected from the snowy winds as it lay inside the cave.

Passing through an entryway in the cave, Maroon could sense the cold air becoming something strange and majestic. Walking deeper into the darkness, Maroon saw a tiny flicker of purple light. Turning a corner in the cave, Maroon saw the light becoming brighter as she entered the room where the purple light surrounded her.

Whoa, Maroon thought. *This place is beautiful, but what's making all this light?*

She took a deep breath and tiptoed forward, blinking against the blinding light. Then, as she got used to the brightness, she opened her eyes wide to see the cause of the magical glow. On the gravel floor by her paws was a purple-like rock, so shiny and bright it was to cast out such color amid the darkness.

A gem! Maroon had heard from her mother how special they were, especially if you found one the exact color of your name. They apparently gave you luck for the rest of your life if you carried it everywhere.

Looking at the gem again, Maroon held her breath, hoping her name would be the same color as this purple gem. Then, leaping with excitement, Maroon barked in joy. The color was indeed a maroon-purple shade, so dark was its color that it was her gem!

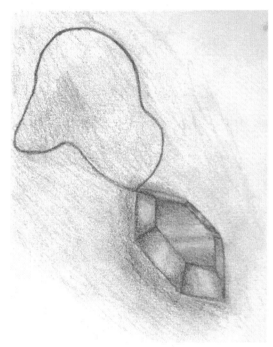

Flicking her tail with pleasure, Maroon barked again with happiness. This was now her gem, and it would be unique to her and bring her luck.

Maroon lowered her head, carefully sniffing at her gem, taking a step forward. Then she lowered her tail in disappointment. How was she going to keep it with her forever?

If it was lying there by itself, she had no way to always have it. Sure, she could always carry it around, but if she was hunting, she would have to set it down, and then she might not find it again. What if she were being chased? If she dropped it, there would be no going back.

She sighed but refused to leave the gem just yet. *Maybe I can bring it with me until I find a way to somehow attach it to me.*

She carefully brought the gem toward her, using her paw, gasping when she suddenly saw something trailing after it.

She quickly brought her paw away from the gem and jumped back, growling at the thing that had just moved. But along with the treasure, it was no longer moving.

Cautiously, she approached the gem again, sniffing. She smelled no living animal nearby.

Slowly reaching out a paw, she scooted the crystal closer to her, and something followed the gem again. Maroon stopped moving the gem. The thing stopped moving, as well. She began moving the treasure again, and the item moved with it.

Maroon lowered her bristling fur as she brought the gem and the mysterious moving thing into view. Relieved, Maroon now knew what had spooked her.

The gem that she now wanted to keep had something connected to it. A small, skinny, brown thread attached to the crystal and went in a loop.

Maroon, first upset about the thread, was now pleased.

Now I have a way to keep this gem with me forever, she thought, feeling thrilled.

Picking up the thread with her teeth, she raised her head. The gem dangled from the rope, swaying in motion. Then she flipped the thread from her mouth onto her nose. She raised her chin and slid the rope down her muzzle until it stopped against her face. Raising her head even higher, she shifted her face, working the thread over her eyes and onto her forehead. Flattening her ears, she slid the rope over them and down her neck. The gem rested against her chest, dangling from the thread that looped around her neck. Satisfaction spread over Maroon. She had gotten what she wanted again.

Maroon stopped smiling. Ever since she'd returned home from her earlier journey, she had gotten everything she wanted, and no one had a chance to get what they wanted.

Maroon hadn't listened to Violet when she'd warned her, and Violet didn't get anything fair out of it but selfishness. When the bears had attacked, Maroon had survived, along with all her friends. She might not have gotten anything she wanted from that, but Slate hadn't gotten what he'd wanted, either—the death of his "friends." Then, when Maroon had decided to leave and go on this long journey, she'd gotten what she wanted. She won the argument with Violet, told everyone about Slate's crime, and had left everything she had ever known to start a new life. She wanted that! Then there was everything that her friends had gotten, which they didn't like. Violet had lost the desperate pleas to keep Maroon from leaving. Thrash had wanted to come with Maroon but was forced to stay home to protect Maroon's friends from Slate. All her friends hadn't wanted her to leave, yet they hadn't gotten what they'd wanted, either.

Maroon lowered her head, upset with herself for not thinking of others. Instead, she was selfish and only thought of herself. But now she had moved on. She would eventually forget about the past and focus on the future.

Maybe next time I see my friends again, this gem will give me luck, she thought, smiling at the thought.

Taking a step forward, Maroon felt something suddenly smack against her chest. Eyes widening, she looked down, only to see her gem. Realization crept over her as Maroon saw that it would sometimes bump against her chest from wild movements because the treasure was on a thread. Still, she would get used to it and eventually not notice it.

She smiled down at her gem and turned to navigate the cave the same way she had come in.

Her eyes had adjusted so much to the darkness that it was almost like walking in broad daylight. Once she walked out of the cave, however, she was blinded by the incredible brightness of white snow and the intense sun.

Blinking and getting used to the daylight, Maroon continued her journey. It wasn't until she passed a couple of bushes that she realized how hungry she had become.

Chapter Nine
The Hunt

The snow crunched underneath her paws as she trotted through the woods. Maroon had passed so much forest, and the area where she had found her gem was far behind her. Head held high, Maroon leaped over a small bush, smiling at the animals she passed by—birds, moles, a mouse or two. Instead of fleeing at her presence, they all stopped and stared, admiring Maroon's gem as it hung from her neck. Maroon grinned. She liked being able to show off her gem to all the other animals.

Maroon realized that the snow-topped trees she passed had more snow than those closer to home. Looking down at her paws, she saw the snow was much higher, too, stopping slightly above her ankles. Maroon shrugged and put less weight on her paws. That way, she would walk more on top of the snow.

Back at home, Maroon remembered being the best at snow walking. She hardly sank into the snow; it was like walking on top of clouds. Maroon giggled when she remembered her friends trying to walk on snow as well as she could but, like most foxes, they all sank into the snow much more than she did. Then it ended in a snow fight with foxes running and yelping in joy, tossing snow at each other and laughing. She smiled at the memory. She also remembered when Slate had joined in the game, laughing and falling into the snow. He'd acted like he enjoyed spending time with them, like they were his friends.

Then why, Maroon began to think, *did he try to kill them all!*

Thrashing her tail, Maroon snarled, hating that her friends didn't believe her. However, she could trust that Thrash would keep them safe from their foolish mistake of not leaving with her.

Maroon couldn't help the feelings of despair. She had left her friends when they'd needed her. She thought the only way to get away from her problems was to run to hide. What kind of friend was she if she couldn't stand up for those she cared about?

The words that Violet had said to her before she'd left repeated in her mind. *If you leave, you're not solving any of your problems.*

Maroon gritted her teeth. Maybe she wasn't solving any of her problems running away like this. She sighed. But was protecting her friends more important than leaving out of hatred?

"Slate!" She began stamping her paws into the snow. "He's the traitor. He's the reason why I left! It's all his fault! He tried to kill my friends! I shouldn't have to run from my enemies! I need to protect my friends from my enemies!"

She raised her head and, at the top of her lungs, shouted, "I'm returning home, and then I'll put an end to the betrayers! Slate, when I get home, I'm going to kill you! And nobody's going to stop me!"

At the last breath she spoke, an animal darted from the bushes and dashed away from her.

Maroon blinked in surprise, having no idea what had happened, but when she stepped forward and saw the animal's paw prints, her hunger rose again.

In the snow were the paw prints of food. More extended paws were in the back, and the smaller paws in the front. Suddenly, Maroon's instinct took over, and she shot after it.

Racing after the creature, she knew what she was chasing. A rabbit!

Jaws parted, heart pounding, she locked sight on the rabbit. Her gem bounced against her chest at the pounding of her paws. Drool slipped from her mouth, and she kicked up snow as she ran.

The rabbit glanced behind then put on a burst of speed when it saw Maroon.

Dodging trees, swerving round rocks and past bushes, Maroon raced on.

The whole forest passed in a blur, and Maroon was only focused on one thing, and she would not stop until she caught it.

Growling, she hurtled herself over a large rock. She was not going to give up yet.

She bounded at some parts of the chase and ran at others. She could feel hot breath rasping out of her nostrils and mouth.

Maroon felt joy. She was able to run free. Was this what adventure felt like? She was the predator hunting down her prey. Her paws didn't sweat because the snow cooled them down. Her pelt burned like fire, but then it was overpowered by the icy chill of the wind. She was hunting, and it felt good.

Putting up another burst of speed, she charged at the rabbit. Then, opening her jaws wide, she breathed in the scent of her food.

The rabbit gasped and ran ahead even faster, but Maroon caught a pleasing scent. It was a female. Maroon almost couldn't tell by the overwhelming scent of fear coming off this rabbit.

The rabbit leaped high, so high it revealed its soft, furry belly. At that exact second, Maroon barked in excitement. There were no holes nearby, no logs, nothing. The rabbit had no chance of escape.

Maroon's tongue slipped out of her mouth, and on she ran, panting extra hard. The thrill of the chase was coming to an end. The rabbit was slowing down, and Maroon was catching up.

A growl escaped her throat as she realized she was getting so close, and she would have something to eat.

Abruptly, the rabbit leaped over a log covered in snow and raced over a solid surface. Maroon followed after but was sent sliding out of control, her chin slamming hard against the ground.

Pain shot through her whole body, and she yelped. She placed her front paws steadily underneath her and, with a push, she began to rise onto her legs. Then her legs slipped and gave way again, and she again landed hard against her chin. Stars danced in her head. This time, she decided to look at where she was instead of putting herself through the pain of trying to get up. Still lying against her chin with her forepaws spread out, she blinked open her eyes.

In great astonishment, she realized where she was. She was still in Maplewood, and she was sure about that from the surrounding trees. But no trees were growing on the solid, smooth surface that she was on now. Instead, she could see snow lining the edges where there was none on the slick surface, and she was facedown, in the middle of a frozen pond.

Looking at the shiny, blue sheet of ice, she knew she had to get off of it, or she could possibly fall through. Knowing it was impossible to stand up on this slippery ice, as she had tried that already, she stuck her front paws out. Digging her claws into the ice, she then hauled herself forward. She kicked out with her back legs as she pulled herself along, hoping it would send her forward a little more.

Puffing as she used most of her strength to pull herself along, she thought back to what had happened. She had been chasing a rabbit. The rabbit must have led her to this ice on purpose to lose her, so she would miss her. Then she remembered the distinct smell of the rabbit, and that it was a girl.

She wants to escape as much as I do, Maroon thought. *If only it was that easy. I've been traveling farther and farther from my problems, and now I might have to go back and face them.*

With rage, Maroon barked, kicking as hard as she could, and flung herself forward.

Spinning in circles, belly to the ground, she slid forward, slowing as she reached the ice's edge.

Raising a paw, she planted it firmly against the snow. Her paw sunk into it, and she could feel the earth beneath. Then, digging her other claw into the snow, she pulled herself forward.

Rising onto shaky legs, she placed the rest of herself onto the snow, relieved to get off the ice completely. Panting heavily after that experience, she laid her head against her paws. Her stomach was empty, her legs were sore from the chase, and she had to pull herself forward on the ice.

"That's it," she breathed. "I've come so far and faced too many challenges. I can't go back. Thrash will kill Slate, anyway, when he finds him acting suspicious. I don't need to go back and face something that's already doomed. I might as well continue on until I find a comfortable home that suits my needs. But first, I'm going to rest. I deserve it, after all."

She rose onto her paws, failing to track the rabbit any further. She stopped under the shelter of some trees.

Piling as much snow as she could into a wall to shelter her, she curled up into a ball and fell asleep, forgetting about the troubled day she'd had.

Chapter Ten
A Journey's End

*I*t's been days since Maroon left. I already miss her, Thrash thought as he looked down, sighing. Then he smiled. He was lying down, resting, and beside him was a sleeping fox.

Thrash couldn't remember her name as she lay with him, but she had a beautiful coat that was almost all black with some bright orange patches and some gray. *Oh, that's it*, he thought. *Her name is Violet.*

He thought back to the first day he had stayed to protect Maroon's friends, right after Maroon had left. He'd hated watching her go, specifically when he couldn't journey with her and help her, but he was glad Maroon trusted him to keep her friends safe.

Thrash remembered the hostile stares the foxes had given him during the first day and how they all had moved to get away from him. He'd tried to spend time with the pups so they would see him as a friend and not a foe, but he couldn't get the puppies to come out of their burrow to play.

So, that first day, he noticed Mahogany jumping up into the air with opened jaws but returning to the ground with teeth closing on nothing. That was when Thrash had decided to help.

She'd gasped when she'd first seen him, but then she'd sat back and watched as he leaped up, closing his teeth around a small beehive hanging from a branch. Then, landing back on all fours, he'd gently handed her the beehive then turned to look back when she'd said *thank you*.

After that, he'd helped her out for the rest of the day. Soon, all of Maroon's friends were enjoying his company, except for Violet. She'd wanted him gone as quickly as she saw him, not trusting him. Whenever he came close, he could sense she was hurting, and not on the outside but on the inside.

She would often sit alone during Magenta's night gatherings. Thrash would follow her and find her over by Maroon's log, her head bowed in pity. She always told herself how she never should have said those things.

When Thrash had approached and asked what was wrong, she'd bowed her head and whined. He'd licked her and told her she could tell him anything. Through grief, she'd told him everything, and he'd listened. She had told him she never should have said some mean things to Maroon and how she shouldn't have let her leave. She wished Maroon and Slate were friends, and Maroon didn't go just because of him.

Thrash understood. He wished Maroon hadn't left, either. After telling Violet that, they had spent the next day together. They'd sat together, telling stories, playing, and laughing. *All to get her mind off of things*, he thought.

Once the day was done, Thrash had remembered telling Violet to go get some sleep, and the following day, he'd come back to check on her.

Violet, Thrash knew, just looked up to him as a friend, and Thrash himself had no feelings for her, either. They were just friends. Besides, a fox and a coyote as mates? Who had heard of such a thing? But thinking about Maroon, he felt … different. He knew what he felt. He loved Maroon.

Being really close to someone and having to see them leave was just too much, Thrash told himself. A*t least now I have a friend here*, he thought, looking down at Violet, who was now rising onto her legs.

Standing up, Thrash watched Violet shake out her pelt then bound away to see Slate. *She trusts him*, Thrash thought, watching Violet jump around Slate. *So do all the rest of Maroon's friends. Maroon is the only one who thinks he's a traitor*. He wasn't sure if he thought Slate was a traitor; he hadn't seen him do anything suspicious.

When Maroon had left, Slate had seemed relieved. Maybe because he didn't want her around if she would just accuse him of betraying everyone. Then he had smiled and shared with his friends, including Thrash, for the rest of the day.

Maybe he isn't a traitor? Thrash thought. *He doesn't act like one.*

Thrash couldn't help it, but he thought of Maroon again. Her red-orange coat, her shining yellow eyes, her black-tipped tail. Thrash had never seen a fox with a black tail before, not until he'd met Maroon.

He knew she was the only fox who had desperately tried to save her friends when there was no hope. He remembered her snapping at him when she'd disagreed with his words. She was so brave, braver than he'd ever been. He looked up to her. He couldn't believe it—a coyote looking up to a fox!—but it was true. He had never felt so inspired when he thought of her. She was the best friend he'd ever had, and now she was ... gone.

He whined. He couldn't bear the thought of never seeing her again. He missed her deeply. He wanted to confess his love to her.

"I can't do this anymore!" Thrash growled, jogging forward. Then, moving away from all the other foxes and approaching Maroon's stream, Thrash stopped, his heart swelling.

This is where Maroon started her journey. He remembered, putting his nose to the ground and locating Maroon's stale scent. *Slate hasn't done anything that would hint he was a traitor, and I miss Maroon so much! They will all be okay if I leave them for a while.*

With those words repeating in his mind, Thrash followed Maroon's trail and left Slate ... alone.

***

Still under the tree, Maroon slept peacefully until snow slipped off a branch and tumbled down onto her. Yelping with fear, Maroon jumped, her bark drowned out by the snow that piled on top of her. All was silent except Maroon's angry yowls when she popped her head out.

"Fox gems!" she swore.

The birds had been enjoying their stay in the trees until they saw the fox's state. Then they flew away, tweeting in a discussion.

"Who do you think you're laughing at?" Maroon hollered in the air. "That's right; fly away!"

Shaking off the snow, Maroon grumbled, "I'm hungry, tired, and I don't feel like stopping, so no one gets in my way unless you want to feed yourself to a starving fox, perhaps?"

Though she knew no small animal was even about to consider giving itself up, Maroon still waited. Then, once it was clear that she would starve again, she stood up and started walking more.

Maroon could feel the cold, snowy winds and its breeze through her pelt as she passed tree after tree. But again, the icy tinge of coldness reminded her about her friends back home.

"I stopped caring about that a while ago!" she growled to herself. "I've decided not to worry about anything I've left and focus on food and shelter."

Making a tremendous leap over a log, Maroon doubled back, holding on to a flickering hope inside her as she peered at any openings. But her hope quickly vanished as she looked at the log's only entrances, buried in a thick mound of grassy earth.

Sighing, Maroon turned away. *No nice warm log for me,* she thought. *Maybe I should keep my eyes open for something else to make a suitable home.*

The trees cleared ahead, and Maroon started sniffing for grubs and tiny bugs to eat. Noticing a small stick, Maroon approached it, clawing at it and wedging her nose to flip it over. Picking it up with her teeth, she moved the twig and found a worm wiggling away. Smacking a paw on the worm, Maroon chewed it up and swallowed it. Though it did not satisfy her hunger, it did cause her to realize she needed more food.

Panting from the effort of her long journey, Maroon stopped walking for a second. She was aching from her head to her tail. It felt like her paws were on fire. She was about to sit when she smelled something tasty.

"Food!"

Rising back onto her paws, Maroon began silently stalking forward. She walked almost on top of the snow as she crept closer. Then, noticing her prey—a fat robin—she realized that it was trying to get a worm by pecking at the snow.

Maroon almost laughed in amusement. *You won't get a worm to come above ground in the snow*, she thought. *I was lucky when I found that worm in that bare patch.*

Still watching the bird, Maroon crouched, waggled her hunches, and then leaped into the air. The bird chirped in alarm and tried to flutter away, but Maroon killed it quickly.

***

For the first time in a long time, Maroon had a full, satisfied belly. The warmth the meat had provided sent strength into her bones. She was going to continue on until she found her new home. But maybe it wouldn't be as easy as she'd thought. Perhaps this whole journey was a waste of effort.

When she turned at a bend of trees, she was rewarded with a remarkable sight. Because she stood on a hill, she could see all that was before her.

Aa snow-coated trapper's cabin, lined with trees and shrubs up to the north. To the south of the house, closer to Maroon, was a small brook. The water, clear and beautiful. To the northeast was tree after tree of forest, snow piled on top of many.

This is home, Maroon thought, gazing in awe at what she saw. *This is my new home.*

Though most birds had flown south by now, the birds that had stayed home for the winter were fluttering around her.

The first thing I'm going to do when I get settled, Maroon thought, looking at her new home, *is drink from that brook.*

With all the new enticing sights and smells luring her in, Maroon started walking toward her new home.

Chapter Eleven
Kitsune

Waking with a yawn, Maroon stretched and sat up. She had found a suitable home, not in a log but in a burrow in a hill, east of the trapper's house. It was surrounded by trees and rocks, and inside her den, it was rather dark and dirty. It was Maroon's first-ever time sleeping in such a burrow, but she found it quite cozy and warm.

Deciding she wanted to explore her territory, she approached the entrance to her den. The sun blinded her eyes just as much as inside the cave. She shut her eyes in a snarl. The sunlight was always around in her log, but in a dark burrow, no light made it in.

Sighing, she made her way outside, enjoying the coolness of snow beneath her paws. She looked around at the trees; this forest was her new home. She breathed in a deep breath of relief. For the first time in a long time, she felt safe and secure. She was as far away from Slate as she could get, and she was in the middle of nowhere. Slate would never find her.

Walking deeper into the woods of her territory, Maroon felt the fresh morning air breeze through her pelt, and the bird song was just as relaxing. So, she continued forward, arriving at the brook. But Maroon didn't want to get that close to a trapper's house before getting a good idea of her new home.

Taking a right, she went on through the forest. Her fur was thick and kept her warm. Then she heard shuffling beneath the snow. She paused and cocked her head, listening. When the sound came again, she took a step, listened, took another step, and listened until she had located the exact spot from where the sound was originating.

She crouched low, wriggling forward to get close to her prey. Then, waggling her haunches, she leaped straight into the air and landed head-first into the snow, jaws closed on nothing.

Yelping with fear and delight, she half-jumped and struggled out of the snow. She hadn't caught anything; her food had probably escaped just in time before the snow had swallowed her whole.

I didn't realize how deep that snow was, she thought. *There must have been a slope in the ground to have piled up that high. Then all the mice and voles relied on deep snow to confuse their predators, as they made tunnels underneath. Well, that's it. I'm not going to make myself look foolish trying that again.*

She looked down at her gem, it was still there, and it had some melted snow on it, which made it sparkle beautifully. *Oh, I love my gem, but I also miss Thrash and all the friends I've left behind.*

As she told herself that, a bird swooped down, enticed by the churned-up snow, clearly not seeing Maroon.

In that second, Maroon sprang forward, clutching the bird in her teeth.

What is it with me and catching birds? she thought. *I guess because it's winter, and I'm going to have to rely on them more. Not all birds travel south.* She left it at that and began helping herself.

Still wandering north from her burrow, she spotted an abandoned shack covered in snow. *Strange*, Maroon thought. *This shack is far from the trapper's house, abandoned. Does that mean it's free for my taking?*

Curious, she strode forward, stopping when she reached the entrance to peek inside. It looked nice. There was no snow inside at all, and it stayed warm, but when she looked closer, she saw a bundle of moss spread out like a nest. Then she noticed the scent; it was a musky smell she had never smelled before.

This isn't abandoned! she realized, starting to back out with fear. But before she could move any farther, she heard a voice.

"You looking for shelter?"

The voice came from inside the shack. In a corner, looking there, Maroon saw a small animal. It was tan-furred, with skinny legs, tiny paws, and a foxlike body and tail. It was way smaller than Maroon, almost the size of a pup, but it was an adult by the looks of it.

Looking at the animal again, she noticed a foxlike bushy tail, but the face confused her. Its face was small and round, its eyes big with a tiny muzzle, but its ears were the most enormous ears Maroon had ever seen for such a small creature. The ears were as wide as its face, with so much fur inside that she couldn't see past it. The ears were as tall as its whole head.

Astonished, Maroon stared at the creature until it spoke.

"Rare fox, you do know it's rude to just stand there." The voice concluded this creature was male and not a pup.

Maroon sputtered, "R-rare?"

The animal raised its head, looking at her in shock. "Of course I said rare. Didn't you ever learn?" he asked, turning to climb atop a wooden box.

Maroon walked cautiously into the shack and sat down on the wood floor, wrapping her tail around her paws. "What do you mean? Why did you call me rare?" she bristled.

After sitting on the box, the creature looked down at her. "You know what rare stuff is, don't you?" he asked.

Maroon nodded. "Who wouldn't?"

The animal replied, "Well, you're rare."

Maroon gasped. "What? Wait. Really? How?"

The animal flicked his tail, beckoning Maroon to look at her own.

When she saw the blacktip, she thought about all her friends who didn't have that back home.

About to explode with excitement, she looked up at the animal, her expression asking if that's what made her rare.

The creature nodded. "Now that we've gotten that out of the way, I'd like to introduce ourselves."

Maroon spoke first, "My name's Maroon. I've come from far away. This place is my home now."

"Ah, a traveler?" he interrupted. "I'm a traveler myself, probably been farther than you've ever known."

"What do you mean?" Maroon cocked her head, "Who are you?"

The animal responded, "My name is Kitsune. I'm a fennec fox from Africa. I was taken from Africa to North America, where we are now, and I was put in a research facility."

"Wow! Why did they take you to the facility?" Maroon demanded.

Kitsune shrugged. "It was because people wanted to learn more about me, so they did research on me."

"How did you end up here?" Maroon scratched her ear.

"I escaped. I ran through the facility's doors and never looked back when I had the chance. I traveled for months until winter came. Where I lived, it never snowed. I wasn't built to survive in this type of weather, so I had to stop traveling. I found this abandoned shack. Though I don't like that it's in a trapper's territory, I'd better make use of it. Then, once spring comes, I'll travel once again until I find a suitable place," he finished.

Maroon sat utterly still. She couldn't believe what Kitsune must have been through. Taken away from his natural home to live somewhere unfitting? She didn't like the sound of that.

"But, if that ever happens to you, you might learn from it." Kitsune opened his small mouth in a yawn. "What did I learn?" he continued. "Different places bring unexpected prizes and problems. I've never experienced winter before. It's cold, which is a problem, but the good thing is that I have large ears, so I can hear voles under the snow."

No kidding, Maroon thought. *Those ears are almost larger than my face.*

"Well?" Maroon jumped at the sound of Kitsune's question. "What's something you learned from your travels?

Maroon thought back to what she had experienced. *I've learned a lot now that I think about it. He is wise; there is no doubt about it.*

Opening her jaws, she spoke, "I learned very well about the forest ever since I left my home. First, I learned that the forest will welcome anything, so always tread carefully. Also, to not be distracted on one thing, or you'll lose focus on another," she remarked, remembering how she had lost the rabbit to the ice. "The other thing I learned is that those you used to trust can betray you." An image of Slate flashed in her mind.

"I like that last one," Kitsune remarked with a grin. His gaze shifted from Maroon to something on her chest.

Maroon's eyes widened as Kitsune stood up, a glint of suspicion in his eyes.

Tension rose as the two stared at each other. Maroon glanced away. Suddenly, with a growl, Kitsune lunged at her.

Chapter Twelve
Trust

Yowling filled the empty air. Maroon felt the desperation of both her and Kitsune. Fur was beneath her teeth that she could not hold for long until it vanished and reappeared with its teeth in her coat.

Maroon turned, snapping at all sides, unable to pin the dashing enemy. Once or twice, she saw jaws open around her gem, but she jumped away before it was enclosed by them.

She heard the sputtering cry of Kitsune, and all replayed itself. Kitsune was trying to take her gem.

Maroon rose onto her back legs with an uproar, kicking out with her front, her teeth bared in warning.

Kitsune leaped onto the box, revealing his fangs and yelping as Maroon swatted her paws out before him. No flesh was torn, but both jumpy animals threatened each other.

Tail following behind, Maroon leaped onto the box Kitsune was on, claws outstretched as she leaped from the ground. Kitsune yowled and puffed with anger, jumping off the box and racing around the room when Maroon had taken his spot.

Now on the upper ground, she corrected her stance upon the box. Then, stiffening her muscles, she raised her head high. Looking down at Kitsune with a stern gaze, who growled in defense, she signaled him to submit.

Kitsune then barked once and sat down, beginning to lick his paws as if nothing had happened.

Burning with rage, Maroon leaped off the box with a yowl and landed on Kitsune. The tiny body wriggled underneath her, but she quickly stood up and firmly placed a paw on his chest, pinning him.

Staring into his calm eyes, she growled, "You forest dog! How dare you try to take my gem! Do you really want to challenge a fox who is bigger than you? Did you want me to look like a fool if you beat me?"

Kitsune only twitched his ear, his expression bored and annoyed.

That made Maroon angrier. *How dare that tiny self think of a strong, powerful fox like me as nothing! I'll teach him.*

"You're a good fighter," a voice croaked.

Maroon looked down at Kitsune, who was smirking with glee.

Stunned, Maroon stepped off him. He got up with a grunt and sat down again.

"That was a fine lesson on trust, wasn't it, Maroon?" Kitsune asked with an awfully toothy grin.

Suddenly, realization swept over her.

That was a test! Maroon sat, surprised. *To test my trust. He wasn't trying to attack me on purpose. It was all a trick!*

Kitsune coughed once, and suddenly, Maroon understood. He was somewhat old. She looked at his frail body and jutting bones. He was rasping a little after his wild movements.

Maroon then felt ashamed, looking at the old fox.

How could I have attacked him? she thought. *He's old, and I should never have made it so rough for him. He was the one who started it, yes, but I should have known that instead of throwing myself into things.*

She sat down. *Maybe that's how I ended up here, in a forest in the middle of nowhere. I don't think. I never think.* She flattened her ears.

"You all right there, little fox?" Kitsune's voice came from behind.

Maroon peeled back her lips and turned to face him. "I'm not little! I'd rather anything bigger than me call me that rather than you." She looked at the tiny fox with disgust. "But even then, I'd rip their tongue out of them to rid me of their rude comments."

Once finished, Kitsune looked at her with shock, and then a smile spread across his face. "You're something, that's for sure. Never met someone like you. Always asking questions yet tough at heart. Always defending yourself, whether fighting or with your tongue."

Maroon sat back with her gaze fixed on the tiny fox.

"Maroon, isn't it? That's a fine gem you have there. Do you mind telling me how you got it?" he inquired.

Maroon opened her jaws to reply then closed them tightly.

Those who you used to trust can betray you. The thought on the lesson that day stuck in her mind. *And I don't completely trust him.*

"I found it. Nothing you should know. And don't mind my asking, but what's in it for you? I found my gem, fair and square. You shouldn't even consider taking it from me, or you'll have no pelt until spring." She had growled that last sentence.

Kitsune laughed. "Don't worry; I'm not interested in something that's already yours. Besides, what does jealousy do except make rivals and leave you in a deep hole?"

Maroon was actually surprised by how valid Kitsune's words were.

He knows a lot, she told herself. *Even if I won't admit it out loud, he's helped me realize what I need to control. I'm too spontaneous, and I need to work on that. I will stop jumping into things and start thinking before I do something.*

"That gem must be special to you then?" Kitsune asked, scratching his ear.

"Well, yes." Maroon looked at her gem. "It brings me luck because it's the same color as my name."

"So, are all foxes named after colors?" Kitsune cocked his head. "Will they all get their own gem?"

Maroon looked at Kitsune, who was waiting for a response. "Yes, all foxes are named after colors, and they don't get their own gems; they have to find one. But it has to be the exact color of their name, or they won't have good luck."

Kitsune grinned. "I guess there's not a gem for me, is there?" He chuckled.

Then Maroon realized, "You aren't named after a color! But every fox is named after a color!"

"Remember, I came from Africa; you live in North America, same as all the other foxes, unlike me. So, how am I, or any of the other foxes who live in Africa, going to hear any of the rules you make up? Well, I simply didn't know," Kitsune finished.

Maroon again realized all the foolish commotion she had made for no reason. "I'm sorry, I didn't realize you never knew about fox names here."

"It's all right, I don't mind. Now I have missed my afternoon nap. It was nice meeting you. Look forward to seeing you around." Kitsune replied, turning to snuggle into his nest.

Maroon stood up. "Goodbye, Kitsune!" *It's much nicer to have him as my neighbor than Slate, that's for sure*, she thought as she walked out of the shack. *I just hope Thrash is keeping my friends safe.*

Then, after passing many trees and piles of snow, she started toward the brook.

It took her a while to reach it, and when she did, she broke into the ice using her paw. Then she began lapping at the water. The ice-cold water soothed her throat.

She sat down and licked her dripping wet paw dry.

I should have told Kitsune why I left. Maybe he would have helped by telling me what I should do. Should I return home? Should I stay here?

With frustration, she buried her head under her paws. She felt like a failure. She had left her friends with a traitor. She didn't even know if they were alive, and she didn't know if she should go back.

"To be honest, I'm too afraid to go back. What will I find? The corpses of all my friends with Slate standing over them? Will they accuse me of being a traitor for leaving them, and will they side with Slate? It's too much; I feel like I have no choice but to stay here." Maroon sighed.

She looked to the right. In the distance was the trapper's cabin, far enough from her den yet in her territory. The brook was the only water source, and it being a walk away from her shelter meant she had to get closer to the trapper's cabin to drink.

I won't spend too much time at this brook, Maroon thought as she started leaving for her den. *He won't have even noticed a fox has moved in by how quickly I'll get a drink. I'll get in and out, and then I can leave the brook to get out of sight of the cabin.*

"I'll make a promise to myself." She put a paw to her gem. "I will not let that trapper know about me." She reached her burrow and settled into her nest. "And I will never return home."

Chapter Thirteen
The Trapper's Cabin

Many days later, the sun rose high in the sky, and a small shaft of light found its way into her burrow to awaken the sleeping fox. Her gem glistened brightly, waking Maroon as she stretched and sat up.

She licked her chops. She was hungry. It was early in the morning, and she thought she would explore the trapper's cabin and get herself something to eat. She checked to make sure her gem was secure around her neck then began to crawl out of her burrow.

The sun warmed her pelt while the snow froze her paws, but she didn't notice this as she walked toward the brook.

"I should name that brook myself," she told herself. "I'll call it The Diamond Waters because it sparkles like my gem." She looked at her swaying purple gem.

She caught a shrew along the way, and as she reached the brook, The Diamond Waters, she lapped at the water's surface. There were many bird songs coming from above. The birds probably wanted a drink, and when Maroon turned away from the water, they flew down to drink and fly away.

Maroon looked at them from the corner of her eye. "I'm not going to eat you. Can't you tell a full fox from a hungry fox?" she mumbled.

Once it became clear to the birds that she was taking no interest in them, they began to gain enough confidence, and they even put their backs to her. Maroon only grunted and carried on. She had no business with birds when she knew exactly what she wanted to do.

She passed many bushes and shrubs with glistening snow, leaving deep gashes in the white covering from her paws. Then, finally, she approached a small bush wall, the cabin not too far from that.

She took a deep breath then pushed her way through the bushes, having been familiar with the thorn bushes at her old home, and emerged, ready to explore.

Shaking off the few snowflakes that stuck to her fur, she sneakily continued toward the cabin.

After a while of suspiciously sniffing the air, she drew nearer to the trapper's cabin.

"I only want to explore this place to get familiar with what's in my territory," she mumbled aloud as she steadily drew closer to the cabin.

She stopped when a clump of snow slipped from a branch, and she remained still for several moments until she thought it was safe to carry on.

It was all quiet. The birds had stopped chirping the closer she got to the cabin. The snow under paw was soft, and a sound was hardly made. Maroon placed one paw in front of the other. Twice, she grew impatient and took a running leap to get closer sooner.

The air was cold, and no other animals were near. A gust of wind almost blew Maroon off her paws, but she steadied herself with a growl.

Hesitation was all around her. Again and again, Maroon wondered if she should turn around and head back to her burrow, but curiosity won.

The closer she got, the more she thought about going back, and the more she stopped to listen.

Her legs and shoulder ached from crouching the whole way, but then, to her relief, she was at the cabin.

Cautiously sniffing the air, she shook herself once more and looked around. Finally, relieved the wind no longer bothered her because the cabin blocked it off. She leaped onto boxes, sniffed around the perimeter of the walls, and even growled when she saw a large, metal box with black rubber paws.

She sat down and violently scratched at her ear. It had started itching halfway through her sneaky approach to this cabin. She raised her head and looked around when her gem swung and hit her.

Then she suddenly smelled a delicious scent waft through the air from the cabin. She circled around the base of the place many times, confused about why the smell was stronger in one spot than the other and where exactly it was coming from.

After barking in frustration, she discovered the smell was coming from an opening inside the cabin. Unfortunately, the gap was too high up for her to reach.

Maroon steadied herself on her hind legs, directly below the space, and took in many deep breaths of the pleasant smell.

It was the smell of meat, and there were also some other smells.

Then Maroon heard the sound of movement inside and yelped in surprise when a door swung wide open, and a human walked out.

Looking out from hiding behind a box, Maroon recognized this human as the trapper who had killed the bear. Maroon could tell the meat smell was even more robust, and to her surprise, she saw the trapper holding an object with food in it.

She watched as the trapper set the object down and called out. Soon, two lumbering, slender animals, bigger than her, bounded out from the cabin and started eating the food in the bowl.

Maroon couldn't see much from behind the box, but she could see what they looked like. They both had long, floppy ears, spindly legs and tails, and were colored white with some brown patches. The two were definitely taller than Maroon, a little taller than Thrash. As they ate, they continuously wagged their tails and yapped many times. Thrash had told her trappers had dogs back at her old home, so these must be dogs.

After the trapper left the two, Maroon took the chance to get away and return to her burrow. But when she lifted a paw and placed it, her paw sank into the snow with a loud crunch. Maroon held her breath as both the dogs stopped to look around, ears raised. Then they both split apart, noses to the ground, and searched for Maroon.

Maroon stayed put behind the box, crouched, heart thumping inside her chest, trying to figure out when to run. Seconds passed by in a heartbeat. Then one dog scented Maroon behind the box. They approached. Maroon couldn't decide what to do fast enough.

As soon as the dog stuck its head around the box, she heard, "There!"

Maroon pushed off the box with a cry of alarm and began to run, sending snow whirling from her paws.

Behind, she could hear barking as the two dogs started after her. Panting with fear, Maroon ran as fast as possible, her mind whirling in confusion. Soon, she heard a bang, and the bark on the tree ahead of her blew into the air.

The trapper has the stick! He's shooting at me! Maroon thought.

Racing on, she could feel the hot breath of the dogs behind her. She started to bound. All her senses and everything around her were forgotten because her focus turned to running from the dogs.

The barking never stopped, nor did the shooting. The snow made running difficult, and when another shot was heard, Maroon knew where to go—straight to her burrow.

***

Running back the way she had come on her long journey to the cabin, Maroon headed for her burrow.

She had gotten further ahead of the dogs, and she could see the bush wall she had gone through earlier. *I could buy some time by going through that,* she thought quickly. *The big dogs might get confused and not be able to follow. Then I'll make a dash for the burrow.*

Racing ahead, Maroon neared the bush wall, ready to dive in, but she heard a snap before she could. Time stopped, and an eerie silence fell over Maroon. Pain shot up her leg like lightning. She was wrenched back by her leg. Her shoulder felt like it would rip off. Her yelp echoed through the forest. She swore Slate could hear it. Then time resumed.

Maroon looked at her paw in shock and unbearable pain. Her paw, smashed and crooked, was held firmly in the jaws of a steel trap.

The searing pain was pulsing through her whole body from her paw. She could see blood coming from her claw caught in the trap, and with all her instincts, she wished she could lick it. Then she heard another bang and remembered what had been happening before she'd stepped into the trap.

With the sound of the trapper's shots and the approaching barking of dogs, Maroon knew she was doomed.

Chapter Fourteen
An Unwelcomed Face

The snow's beautiful white coat was stained with blood. It was hardly any, though. Maroon had just stepped into the trap, unable to move and in unbearable pain. She was crouched low in front of the bush wall, barking ringing in her ears. Unable to free her paw from the trap, she had to wait for the dogs and the trapper to finish her off.

Maroon had second thoughts as the barking grew closer. She tried yanking her paw out of the trap, sending new waves of pain through her body.

She allowed herself to close her eyes and think of something pleasant before being killed.

"Goodbye, Thrash," she whispered.

Then there was a holler of anger and the sound of a small animal leaping in front of her. Maroon opened her eyes in shock at what she saw.

It was Kitsune. He had jumped in front of her, protecting her from the dogs.

What's he doing? Maroon growled the thought. *He's going to get himself killed. The dogs are so much bigger than him!*

But then, as soon as the dogs appeared and spotted Kitsune, he began to run, calling out for the dogs to give chase, and they did just that.

Not even stopping to check their surroundings, the dogs started after Kitsune, not noticing Maroon. Kitsune led the dogs and the trapper away from her. Then the forest went silent, but pain still throbbed in her paw, as if she had been bitten repeatedly.

Maroon moaned pitifully. She was pinned to the ground like a squashed bug, unable to remove her paw from the trap as it sent burning pain through her. She forgot to breathe every now and then, thinking breathing would worsen the pain. She whined and chewed fiercely at the trap, longing to stop the pain and run home with all her might. Only after pain shot through her teeth did she stop, licking away the metallic taste in her mouth. She again tried to pull her paw out, but even anger wasn't enough to ignore the pain.

Where is Kitsune? Maroon wondered. *I hope he's okay. He saved my life.* Maroon thought the small fox was so wise, though sometimes he annoyed her greatly with all the unnecessary questions he asked. But she wouldn't want him to die, would she? No, she didn't want to lose the only friend she had here.

She tried not to think of Violet's upset face when she had left, how it had hurt to leave them.

"And I might never see them again." She rested her head on her paws, sighing. "If I'm dead."

***

Though Maroon didn't suspect several hours had passed, it felt like it had. There was still no sign of Kitsune or the dogs.

I hope Kitsune used his wisdom to his advantage, she thought.

There was no sound of birds chirping or anything else to comfort her. She couldn't even quench her parched throat. Her breathing was slow and calm.

Maroon didn't object to death. In fact, she would rather die by a trap than a dog. She breathed in what she thought was her last breath and closed her eyes.

Then she raised her ears in alert when she heard paw steps approaching. But these paw steps were smaller and lighter sounding. *Could Kitsune have returned?* she thought with inference. But the paw steps were made by an even smaller animal than Kitsune. She sniffed the air and discovered it was a rabbit.

Soon, a tiny, long-eared animal appeared cautiously from the bushes, nose twitching and eyes blinking curiously. It hopped over to Maroon. Its gray fur made Maroon think she had seen this rabbit before.

It's the female rabbit I failed to catch! Maroon remembered. *I only lost it because it led me to the frozen pond.*

The rabbit approached with caution, stifling a smile.

Maroon thought she was dreaming. Then she growled and sprang at the rabbit. It shrank away with a shriek, and Maroon's leg yanked her back. She yelped and threw herself at the trap in pure rage, desperately biting and clawing at it, trying to free her paw.

When she finally gave up, Maroon sat up, her ears flattened, panting. She managed a soft whine.

The rabbit noticed this and seemed to flatten its ears in pity then hopped away.

Maroon didn't want to be left alone again, especially when she knew she would die.

With a soft crunch of snow, the rabbit returned, bringing a large piece of meat with it.

She must have stolen that from the dogs! Maroon realized. *So, they must still be out there, hunting Kitsune!*

The rabbit set the meat close enough for Maroon to reach without letting Maroon get close to her. Maroon grabbed the flesh with a growl of surprised thanks, chewing it slowly, using her free paw to help keep it in place. She ate the meat and felt a boost of energy and strength go through her.

While she ate, she noticed the rabbit scoot a strip of wood filled with water next to her, and Maroon began to drink that.

She's helping me, Maroon thought. *Even after chasing her to the ice and almost killing her, she's still helping me.*

The rabbit and Maroon sat and looked at each other for a while before the rabbit knew she had made the fox's day better, and she could do no more.

Maroon, watching the rabbit turn away, said, "Thank you." But the rabbit had already left.

After sitting for some time, long after the rabbit had fed her, Maroon stood, ears alert, still with one paw in the trap. She heard paw steps, and they were getting closer. Maroon's fur rising, she yelped in surprise when she saw who had just come through the bushes, and her whole body filled with rage.

"Maroon? Maroon! Oh, I was looking for you! But, I—" He stopped short and gasped when he saw her in the trap.

Maroon's growl rose and, at last, she couldn't take it anymore.

"What do you want, Slate?" she growled. "Did you come to kill me?"

Slate stood, shocked for a moment, then sat down. "What?"

"Don't act stupid!" Maroon lashed out, trying to tear him apart, only to yelp when her inflamed paw was moved. "I know you, and I've known what you've done. Thrash couldn't stop you; you must have killed him. You killed everyone back home, and now you've come to kill me. Then you will go somewhere knowing you got exactly what you wanted *again*!"

For a moment, Slate looked speechless.

I've done it. I've read Slate's mind, she thought.

But then he looked hurt.

"Why would you say that?" he yowled.

The pain in Maroon's paw was growing ever worse, and she sunk down in exhaustion. "Go ahead, finish me," she croaked.

"What?" Slate said, taking a step toward her.

"I know you want to. You always have." She coughed.

Slate lowered his head. "Maroon, I ... I am not going to kill you."

Maroon groaned, "I should've known. You want me to die like this. Ha! Good choice. I'd rather die like this than from you!"

Slate growled and cuffed her ear. "That's enough, Maroon! Stop it! You are being ridiculous! You think just because you hate me means I hate you?"

Maroon raised her head. "Say that again?"

"Look, I know you hate me, and you expect me to hate you, too, but I think you're cool. You're fun and smart. Why would you ever say such a thing?" Slate finished.

Maroon hadn't realized her jaw had been parted and quickly shut it. "Is this some kind of trick?" She laughed.

Slate cuffed her ear again. "Maroon! I'm not going to kill you. If there's one thing we need to get straight, it's this." He cleared his throat. "I never caused the bear attack."

Maroon was shocked to silence. *What does he mean? With all the evidence ...?*

Slate sat down and looked at her with a pleading gaze. "Will you let me talk?"

Maroon revealed her fangs. "I guess."

Slate took a deep breath then began. "It was the first time I smelled the bears' scent, I didn't know what it was, so I told everyone about it. I knew I had to keep you all safe, so the next day, I told Violet that I was going hunting and that she shouldn't follow me. I ... I didn't want her to get hurt, so I went hunting and caught a bird. When I found the bears' ambush. I was so scared that they almost killed me, but I ran away. Then I realized what they were doing, and I tried to stop them. I tried to talk it out, but they barged into camp, and I knew I had to do something. So, I ran into the woods, looking for help, and found it."

Maroon gasped. "The trapper?"

Slate nodded. "Yes, I saw the trapper and got him to chase me. Unfortunately, he lost me, but he was led to the bears by the commotion.

"I watched as a bear got shot, hoping that was how it would end, and it was. The bears ran away, and I returned with my prey, hoping to feed anyone who needed it. That's when it all went downhill. You called me a traitor and gave a list of reasons how I was one. You stated that I wasn't there when the attack started and that meant that I knew it would happen. It hurt so much to know someone hated you and wanted you dead. You wouldn't have known." Slate stared at his paws.

"Oh, Slate," Maroon said in stupidity. "I'm sorry."

Slate raised his head. "You really mean that?"

Maroon growled. "Well, I mean, I'm sorry for thinking of you as a traitor. I should have asked for your side of the story first.

But that doesn't mean I don't hate you anymore. On the contrary, I still don't really like you."

"Oh." Slate pawed at the ground. "Well, thank you, but that's not why I have come."

Maroon's doubts started to come back, and she tried to stand. Her paw was in so much pain that she couldn't, and she sank back into the snow with a yelp.

Slate closed his eyes as if he couldn't bear to look at her. "I'd like to get your paw out of the trap first. If you don't mind?"

Maroon paused. As much as she did hate him, even after she believed he wasn't a traitor, she didn't want him to touch her.

"Fine!" she snarled. "But make it fast."

"I'll try." Slate stood up and fastened his teeth around one jaw of the trap. Then he put his paw on the other to try to pry it open. Instead, he pushed one of the trap's jaws down. Then, without waiting for Slate to open the entrapment any wider, Maroon yanked her paw out of the trap with a feeling of relief and pain, and tumbled back into the snow.

Slate came to help her up, but she snapped at him and growled, keeping her injured paw against her chest.

Slate sat down again. "Do you have a safe place somewhere we can stay so that I can tell you my news?"

Maroon stopped licking her paw and gestured with her head toward the bush wall. "I have a den just east of here."

Slate smiled, "Let's go there."

Chapter Fifteen
The News

Wincing with every step, Maroon trudged back toward her burrow, with Slate following behind. Every step caused her to limp even more. Finally, she sank deep into the snow, her head spinning and pain throbbing in her paw.

She heard Slate's paw steps approaching her from behind as she gasped for air.

"Maroon? Here let me help," he spoke.

Maroon growled, "I don't need help from an enemy. Even if you aren't a traitor, I still don't want your pity!"

Slate yapped in amusement then spoke, "Maroon, it's obvious you need help. Anyone can see that."

With an annoyed snort, Maroon allowed herself to be helped up and leaned against her enemy for support. Together, they began toward her burrow.

***

It felt weird inside a den with Slate, but Maroon would make herself deal with it until he told her his news. Then he would be gone.

Quickly licking her paw, Maroon lay, ears pricked, listening to Slate's words.

Why couldn't Thrash have come instead? Maroon griped to herself. *I'd rather anyone else have seen the mess I caused back at the cabin than Slate.*

As she lay on the soil, licking her paw, Slate approached her, sniffing at the open wound he could smell. Maroon stopped licking and growled, ears pinned back and fangs showing. Slate noticed Maroon's defensive behavior and turned to sit on the other side of the den.

The loose dirt hung tightly to the walls of the burrow; the cool air swept past outside, unable to reach the warm air inside the den.

After a repetitive licking cycle, Maroon raised her head. "So? Get on with it!"

Slate had relaxed and was surprised when Maroon first spoke.

"I, um …" He cleared his throat.

"I said get on with it, slug!" Maroon snapped.

Slate yowled. "I'm going, okay?"

Maroon grumbled and continued her licking.

Slate took a breath and began, "The news I have is about ba—"

"Hold on," Maroon cut him off. "Can we talk about how you found me? I thought Thrash was watching you. Unless you told him you were innocent?"

"Well, I'll get to that," he answered.

"I want to know now!" Maroon growled so loudly that she almost thought a bear was nearby.

"Okay, I followed your scent."

"*How*?" Maroon snapped her head up, roaring in rage. "What was the point of leaving if you were just going to follow me?"

Slate pawed at the ground. "Well, can you listen?"

Maroon growled again. "I just wasted so much of my winter!"

"Maroon, please!" Slate cried out louder than her. "Can you just listen?"

Maroon sighed and laid her head on her paws. She wanted to hear the news, didn't she? How was she going to if she kept breaking into sudden outbursts?

"Fine," she growled. "Tell me everything."

Slate's eyes widened, and he opened his mouth to speak. A bird called from outside and interrupted him. After she growled at him again, he began. "Before winter, you left. Many days after that a"—he paused, swallowing hard—"a pack of wolves invaded.

They took over the camp, attacking everyone and claiming our territory. I didn't want them to kill me, so I ran away. I don't know if anyone else escaped, but I followed your trail. Eventually, I caught up to you. You have to come back, or all your friends will try to take on the wolf pack, and all of them will die." Slate looked at the ground.

Maroon leaped to her paws, but then she crumpled to the ground in pain when she put weight on her injured leg. Ignoring the sharp pain, she stared at Slate, eyes large with worry and shock.

"What color was the alpha wolf?" she demanded, sitting back up with her paw tucked tightly against her chest.

"White with cold, yellow eyes," Slate said, shivering. "At the time of the attack, his eyes met mine, and they seemed to read every inch of me, as if he knew everything I was thinking, deep into my soul."

Maroon could only gape at him as shivers ran down her spine. She remembered the first time she had seen the Alpha's eyes and how unsettling they were.

Maroon shook her head violently, trying to clear her head of those terrible memories.

"I have to go there now! I have to help them!" Maroon jumped onto three legs, keeping her injured front paw above ground.

"No!" Slate growled, springing in front of the den entrance. "You can't go back until—"

"Get out of my way!" Maroon snarled.

"No! Maroon, you can't. It's too dangerous to barge into wolf territory! We have to get past the wolves and find everyone; make sure they are all safe. Then we can all find a new territory."

"And surrender ourselves and our territory to the wolves? No way!" She sprang at Slate, who ducked and fled the burrow entrance. She followed him, limping.

"Maroon, no!" Slate growled, standing in front of her. "Maroon, listen! You do want to protect your friends, don't you?

How will you do that if you leap in and start attacking the wolves? If you're killed, who will save your friends then?"

Panting, Maroon stood, looking at Slate, closing her parted jaws. Finally, she realized he was telling the truth.

If she went into wolf territory without a plan, as she had wanted to do with the bear attack, it could end badly.

"You're right," she said in disgust. "I'll go and save my friends, but I'll make a plan before charging in."

"Great!" Slate barked, foolishly wagging his tail. "Let's go!"

Maroon straightened and snapped at him, "Hold on! Whoever said we were going together? I would rather you stay here, and I'll go save my friends without your help!"

Slate sat down and cocked his head. "Well, Maroon, what will happen when you leave me here to go save your friends and come back? Well, I'll still be here, waiting for you, even barking in your face with all the questions that I would have. Or, if you take me with you, we could get rid of the wolves, and you could travel back here without ever having to see me again. So, which one do you want?"

Maroon paused again, annoyed by how wise his words were. *I don't want to see him ever again, do I? Even if leaving without him means I won't have someone telling me what to do, I'd have to force him to go when I return. At least I'll get a lot of free time on that journey. But, if I take him with me and leave him at my old home, I will feel better on the trip back here.*

She sighed. "Fine, come on. There's no time to lose."

***

Maroon was lying, sprawled upon the dirt in her burrow, licking her paw.

It felt so much better after she had taken care of it all afternoon. The blood of her injury was gone, leaving only an open wound.

Maroon had to be thankful that Slate had gotten her out of the trap. Thrash had told her of animals dying in them. They were unable to move. Like Thrash had said, they had to wait for death.

She stopped licking her paw, sighing as she waited for Slate to come back from hunting.

After we wake up tomorrow, we'll leave, she thought. *The sooner we get to the wolves, the better. Then I can come back here without ever seeing him again.* She was proud to rethink Slate's words only because they meant the truth.

Pricking her ears, she heard Slate pad into the den, bringing a bird and two voles with him.

"All right," he said, remoistening his tongue after setting down the prey. "Here, you take the bird—you need the most prey to help bring energy back into your body." He pushed the bird over with his nose.

Ugh, I'm so sick of birds, Maroon thought as she became annoyed.

"And I'll have these two voles." He smiled.

"What's with the enthusiasm?" Maroon growled. "I'm not a huge fan of positivity."

"I can tell," Slate mused.

"Excuse me?" Maroon snapped her head up.

"Oh, uh, you're very nice, yes," he said stupidly.

"Uh, someone help me. I don't know how much longer I can take with you." She rolled her eyes.

"Oh, you won't have to worry. When you get tired of me, I'll expect you to rip off my pelt," Slate joked.

Maroon replied, "Oh, I'll look forward to doing just that."

Then they both broke out in laughter, stopping themselves quickly.

Maroon took a bite into her prey. The bird tasted good, and she slowly but gradually got her strength back as she ate.

After the two had eaten their fill, Maroon growled at herself for laughing at Slate's stupid joke. If she wanted to survive anywhere near him, she had to be as mean as possible. Maroon needed Slate to submit to her so she could make all the decisions.

Settling into a leaf nest that she had created earlier, she laid her head on her paws, making sure Slate slept on the other side of the den. With a heavy-hearted sigh, she closed her eyes and drifted off to sleep.

Chapter Sixteen
An Enemy's Journey

The journey with Slate started off awful. Slate wouldn't stop talking and gossiping, but he also recited poetry, and Maroon hated it.

She had told him to stop multiple times, but he wouldn't. He continued on with his poetry.

"The sky is blue … Hmm, that could work. What else could work? Well, one thing I know is that you and I will enjoy this journey." He wagged his tail.

"Oh, shut up!" Maroon found it more annoying to have a fox mention her than the poetry itself. "Stop talking! First of all, no, we will not enjoy this; and secondly, I told you to stop several seconds ago!"

"Oh, sorry. I should have stopped before I made you angry," he said, looking at the ground.

"Well, I don't care! All I care about is having some peace and quiet because we have a long way ahead of us!" Maroon replied, continuing on a limping pace.

Instead of going back all the way Maroon had come, Slate had insisted on going a different route back home to keep clear from the cabin.

As they walked through the dense trees and snow, Slate stopped and lay down, panting vigorously.

"Oh, what foolishness is this? I'm the injured one, and I've come farther than you," Maroon complained as Slate collapsed with exhaustion. "What even is this? Get up!" She turned to snap.

"S-Sorry, I …" *Pant.* "Need." *Pant.* "Rest," Slate rasped.

After recovering his breath, he said, "I'm sorry. You were going too fast, and there was snow making it hard to keep up, and—"

"What?" Maroon growled.

"Oh, I, uh … I can't run or go too fast for very long because it gets hard to breathe, and my throat—"

"Oh yeah, there's something wrong with you," Maroon grunted, continuing on, not waiting for Slate to catch up.

"Well, my mother never said it was wrong. She said it made me special because no one else in my family has it—"

"Yup, that means there's something wrong with you," she interrupted.

"My mother always made me feel better after my brothers' teased me. She was nice that way," he spoke, coughing every few seconds.

"You still talk about your mother?" Maroon snorted. "That's weird."

"Well, yes?" Slate seemed confused. "Anyway, she always told me to be nice to others, and they will be nice to you. But so far you haven't been very nice to me," Slate rambled.

Maroon glared at him. "How old are you?" she asked.

"Well," Slate responded, "how old are you?"

"Rude!" Maroon snapped. "Everyone should know it's rude to ask someone their age."

"Then, why did you ask me?" Slate mused.

"Yeah, okay!" She cuffed his ear. "Don't turn this back on me!"

"Well, if you really want an answer, I'm one years old."

"Me, too, though I'm almost two," Maroon replied.

"Maroon, you have not had kits, have you?" Slate asked.

Maroon turned around instantly. "What? No. Why?"

"Oh, I was just wondering because you've been treating me like a kit this whole time. You know I'm not a kit, right?" He stopped to scratch his neck.

"Okay, well, I'm treating you like a pup because you're acting like one." She smacked her tail into his face. "Also, today,

I'm not as grouchy as yesterday. I almost died, so don't blame me. But can you please just be quiet for a while?"

Slate responded, "Oh, sure, I do not usually talk this much, but I never got to talk to you before."

Maroon sighed. "Yeah, well, if you keep it up, you know what I'll be pleased to do."

Slate, eyes closed and grinning in amusement at her joke, said. "Oh, right. Okay."

The two continued on their journey back home to save her friends.

Slate stopped about two more times to catch his breath. They had barely gotten far from the trapper's woods, and Maroon didn't like the little amount of ground they were covering.

"This is taking too long!" Maroon grumbled. "If you would quit stopping every now and then and stop talking, we would have already been four times farther than this!"

"Look, I'm sorry." Slate stopped walking to pick up a pine cone. "I just want to enjoy this while we can."

"We are going on a journey to save our ... *my* friends from being eaten by wolves! What do you mean you want to enjoy this?" Maroon smacked the pine cone away.

Slate gave a gasp as he watched it disappear over a snow-coated bush.

"Maroon, I'm sorry. I really am! I just—"

"You've said *I'm sorry* a thousand times!" Maroon interrupted him, "but yet you keep doing something that annoys me. It's like you're doing it on purpose."

Slate averted his gaze. "Okay, I'll stop getting distracted, and I'll try to keep up!"

Maroon mumbled, "I'll be glad when this journey is over."
She could hear Slate speak behind her.

"Maroon, would you like to hear a story?"

"Oh no!" She turned. "Don't even start, okay? Do not!"

Slate grinned. "Once upon a time—"

"No! Stop. I don't want to hear a story!" Maroon cried out.

"Two foxes had to go—"

"No!" Maroon cried out again. "Slate, listen, if you start, I will be greatly annoyed."

But Slate, finding it amusing, continued, "And they didn't get along."

Maroon sighed and grinned. She knew she didn't like Slate, but she would let him enjoy himself for a bit. Also, she had no choice. So, Slate continued to annoy Maroon.

Chapter Seventeen
Friend or Foe

Maroon awoke from her sleep. She saw a streak of purple and orange as the sun set in the sky. *Good*, she thought. *I like night.*

Getting up from under a bush, she looked for Slate, but he was not under the tree.

"Where is he?" she thought aloud. "I thought I left him here."

Getting up, she saw deep paw prints in the snow. She followed them.

After walking through a shrub, Maroon grumbled, "I should really keep him tied to a vine rope. That way, he won't wander out of my sight."

Once she was in an open clearing, she found him. He was up in a tree.

"What do you think you are, a squirrel?" Maroon taunted.

Slate turned his head to look at her, his gaze demanding silence.

Maroon quickly shut her mouth when she saw a bird.

The bird was now watching Maroon, seeming to tease her for not being able to reach it, not knowing Slate was behind it.

Maroon smirked. *Oh, it's in for a bit of a surprise.*

At that moment, Slate sprang from his branch and onto the bird without making a sound, pinning it with two little paws.

After killing it, he picked it up in his jaws and shuffled down the tree trunk headfirst.

"What was that?" Maroon asked after he set the prey down in front of her.

"What? The climbing?" He licked his chops. "Oh, that was hunting."

"But you're a fox, not some squirrel." Maroon twitched her tail.

"Well, I'm a gray fox. I am about the size of a fisher. Have you ever seen a fisher?" he asked.

Maroon shook her head. "No."

"Yeah," Slate started to explain, "that's because they have been hunted so much for their fur that they almost went extinct. But, as a gray fox, I basically take their place, hunting in the trees."

Maroon was impressed. "Wow, do you think you could do that again?"

Slate looked around. "Well, there is no prey out, but I will show you how I climb."

He sprang up and dashed to the nearest tree. Digging his claws easily into the bark, he quickly shuffled up onto a branch. Then he sprang from tree to tree with a running leap, digging his claws deep into each branch. The forest animals went silent when they saw Slate in the trees.

Gripping onto the trunk of a tree, he jumped down headfirst.

After he landed, a snowflake fell on Maroon's nose.

"As if there's not enough snow already. Fox gems!" She sighed, picking up the bird.

Slate came bounding up to her, panting. "If you noticed, I don't get tired in the trees because there is no need for long-distance running like there is on the ground, or nothing slowing me down like snow. I am mostly climbing, anyway."

Maroon growled with prey in her jaws, "Sure, whatever. Can we just get out of here now?"

Slate cocked his head. "Uh, I suppose so."

He led the way, with Maroon following behind, toward the shelter of the forest.

"So, you don't like the snow?" Slate asked as they approached the trees.

"Well, I do." Maroon wasn't about to mention how she had played in the snow earlier on her journey. "I just don't really like being actively snowed on, especially while trying to take care of an injury."

"I understand," Slate spoke. "I am not a fan of snow myself. I am not really made for it. But when we find a log or burrow, we should be fine."

After walking through the forest as it snowed, following Slate, Maroon spotted a fallen tree ahead, positioned upright enough to create a shelter.

"There," she mumbled through feathers. "Up ahead."

"What?" Slate squinted, looking straight. "Oh yeah, I see it now. Come on!" He bounded forward, desperate to leave the snowfall, and leaving Maroon to hobble behind.

When she got to the tree entrance, Slate was sitting by the opening, welcoming her inside.

She ducked down and went in, not noticing Slate's flattened ears as she ignored him.

Coming in behind Maroon, Slate took the prey from her and politely set it on the dry leaves found under the tree.

Maroon settled down, too tired to care how damp the leaf bedding was.

Slate shook the melting snowflakes off his pelt and dug around in the leaves.

With the wind blowing and the snow falling, Maroon started to shiver. Her body cold and her paw throbbing with pain, she found it difficult to fall asleep. And, when a gust of wind passed, Maroon couldn't help but let out the chatter of teeth, fur fluffed up.

She heard the crunch of dead leaves as Slate stood over her. With bedding in his jaws, he laid it down on and around Maroon. It felt strange, but it brought some of her warmth back.

"Do you mind?" Slate asked, pawing at the ground next to her. "You'll freeze by yourself."

Opening an eye to glance at him, Maroon breathed deeply. *Sleeping beside my enemy. I never thought this would ever happen. But what he said is true; I will freeze if I don't get warm.*

"Fine," she mumbled sleepily.

She could hear the rustle of bedding then felt Slate's pelt brush hers. After he settled against her, she instantly felt warmth inside her. Opening her eyes, she saw Slate curled up beside her, ears flicking, almost asleep.

He's much better when he's asleep, she thought. *He always acts safe around me, like he can't take care of himself for too long.* She felt guilty about snapping at him, but enemies would always be enemies. There was no changing that. Of course, if one of her friends were here, she'd much rather have one of them take Slate's place. At the moment, however, it wasn't possible. Closing her eyes, she enjoyed the warm comfort and drifted to sleep.

***

Waking with a yawn, she raised her head and looked at the ground before her. There lay a dead vole and the bird Slate had caught yesterday. Besides those was a variety of fruits. She could see red and blackberries, along with mushrooms. There was no sign of Slate.

Getting up with a grunt, Maroon sniffed at the berries then took a bite of a few. Then, limping out into the sunlight, she looked for Slate.

The sun's rays turned her red-orange pelt to a glowing bright golden color.

"Slate?" she called out, glancing to the left and right.

"I'm here!" he called back.

She turned to look at him. He was at the edge of the clearing, gaping at her in shock. Then, shaking his head, he trotted over to her.

"M-Maroon! I didn't know it was you. I, well, your fur was just—"

"Enough," Maroon interrupted him. "Where did you find those berries?"

Slate thought for a split second then replied, "I found them in a raspberry patch. It was not touched by the snow because there was a log."

"Okay, that's good." Maroon turned to walk back into the shelter.

Slate followed her, averting his gaze after the second time she had ignored him.

Entering the shelter, Maroon made her way to the prey, picking up the vole and eating it.

Slate came in after her, pushing the bird over to her.

"I'm not eating that." Maroon stopped chewing to speak. "I've had bird more times than you can count. Besides, I'm already eating this vole."

"No," Slate said. "I want you to eat both. You need it more than I do, and I am the one who can still hunt, so please, take it."

Maroon grumbled but took the bird, anyway.

When Slate left to go hunting again, Maroon tried to go outside. However, when she stood up, keeping her left paw above the ground, her head spun.

Dizzy and confused, she sank to the ground. An itchy sort of pain rested in her paw. Muscles tense and faint, she called out to Slate, but her voice caught in her throat. Tongue lolling, she could see foam forming around her mouth. Fuzzy-eyed, her heart also pounded. Blackness swarming around her, she could feel nothing. Nothing at all.

Chapter Eighteen
Survival

"Maroon? Maroon!"

The voice sounded distant.

Maroon's head swam, and everything was blurry when she opened her eyes. Everything felt like a dream, and she closed her eyes again in exhaustion.

"Maroon! Wake up, please!"

She heard the cry again. Reopening her eyes, she saw Slate. His eyes were wide in horror, and his fangs showed in confusion. Then he slammed both paws against her ribs in desperation.

The pain felt like an echo in her mind, slowly fading out of existence. She could barely feel his fur brush against hers.

"Maroon, no! Wake up! You have to!" Slate's voice was becoming quaky. "Maroon, do not die on me," he whispered. Then Slate shoved Maroon onto her right side with a grunt.

Her consciousness slowly returning, with a gasp, Maroon rolled back into a crouch, still drowsy.

"Maroon!" Slate exclaimed, jumping up to nuzzle her but quickly stopping himself. "Maroon, your paw—it's infected," Slate told her, studying her expression. "Here, you need food and water. Maybe I can find something to heal your paw, but right now, you need strength." He then dashed out of the burrow, leaving Maroon confused and sick.

Maroon kept her head raised, nipping at her tail when she was close to sleeping. She didn't understand why she was refusing to nap. All she knew was to wait until Slate came back.

Not long after he left, Slate returned. In his jaws, he carried a squirrel. He put it under Maroon's nose and forced her to eat. Slate wouldn't leave her alone until she had eaten all but fur and bones.

Then he dashed out again, returning with an icicle, which he let melt into her mouth, doing his best to ignore the freeze that it caused him.

After Maroon had eaten and had enough water to drink, Slate let her sleep. He curled next to her and rested his tail on her, keeping her warm and not leaving her side until she was ready to wake up again. Then he would bring her more prey and look for a healing herb of some sort.

After many naps, Maroon awoke to a tingling but soothing feeling in her paw. She looked through squinted eyes to see a green plant wrapped around her paw. She could smell the scent of torn herbs and guessed the herb had been cut, the poultice resting on her wound.

Then she saw Slate gagging and constantly licking his chops while muttering about how awful it tasted. She sank back into a slumber.

***

Waking refreshed for the first time in a long time, Maroon looked around. Her paw was sore, but she noticed it felt much better. Looking down at it, Maroon saw the herb was gone, and the skin around her wound was slowly healing. *It must not have been healing before*, she realized. *I wasn't doing it any good when I kept pushing myself onward.*

She began to lick at the wound, only to snap her head back when she tasted the rancid taste of an old herb poultice.

Approaching paw steps came from outside, and she looked at the entrance of the tree shelter. It was still winter, but she didn't know how much time had passed when she had been asleep.

Slate bounded in, shivering and shaking snow from his pelt. When he saw her, his eyes lit up, and he dropped the prey he was holding.

"Maroon! I am so glad you are feeling better! Here, I brought you something." He dropped yet another bird at her paws.

"Thanks," Maroon said, sitting up. "How long was I asleep?"

Slate scratched his ear. "Oh, just a day and a night. I made sure you got better, though."

"I can't remember much," Maroon said, though she did remember one thing—Slate never left her side, even though they were enemies.

Standing on three legs, Maroon waved her tail in determination. "Can we go now?" she asked. "I'd like to get back home soon."

"It will be a while," Slate spoke. "We are still far away, and I want you to pass this sickness before you start walking again."

"Fine." Maroon lay down again. "I'll stay, but only until I'm better."

Slate sat down beside her, but Maroon was too tired to care.

"Maroon, would you like a story?" Slate asked.

Maroon half-growled, half-mumbled, yet she let Slate talk.

"Once upon a time, there was a bird that couldn't fly," Slate began.

Maroon closed her eyes and listened carefully to each word Slate said. She never liked when Slate talked, but she enjoyed his story at this moment.

"The bird always tried to fly but never could, but he still practiced. Animals always teased him for trying when he knew it was impossible, but the bird ignored them and kept trying."

Maroon could feel something tighten around her neck and realized her gem was still there. She had almost forgotten about it.

"The bird never gave up, even when he fell out of a tree while practicing. He would just pick himself back up. He would help other birds learn to fly when he was not practicing. Even if he could not show them how, he would tell them how. He would describe what flying must feel like, describing it so well that all the birds he taught wanted to fly. He taught them to believe in themselves, and they could fly," Slate continued. "Then, because he did so many good deeds to others, a good deed was returned to him, and that good deed was his ability to fly." Slate finished his story and looked at Maroon, but Maroon was already asleep, with a smile on her face.

Chapter Nineteen
Traveling Once Again

Waking without a sign of illness, Maroon started limping to the shelter's exit.

Slate was still curled up asleep, so she grabbed him by the scruff and yanked him awake, dragging him across the ground.

Slate scrambled to his paws and gently pushed Maroon away, forcing her to release him.

Maroon turned and began limping outside, signaling for Slate to follow. "Come on, slug; hurry up. I want to go home and save my friends!"

"Whoa! Wait for me!" Slate sped to catch up. "If you keep up with this pace, I will die of exhaustion."

Maroon snickered. "I guess I wouldn't want you to die, would I?" She slowed down.

There was silence between them until Slate finally spoke. "So, your paw must feel better?" he asked hopefully.

Maroon responded, "Yes, much better. I can actually put weight on it now. Before, I couldn't even walk on it." She paused to look at him. "Thanks to you."

"Well, you are welcome. I want you to see your friends as soon as possible, and if it means stopping to rest and heal, it is worth it."

Together, they headed on farther into the forest, on a quest to return home.

***

Maroon, trudging through the snow, looked up above her head and into the trees. Slate was running through the treetops better than he could on the ground.

A stick fell and hit Maroon. She yelped, and Slate dove down from the branches to ask if she was okay as he repeatedly apologized.

"I'm fine," she spoke. "I'll get you back, though."

Slate stayed on the ground.

It was taking much longer to return home than Maroon had thought it would. When she'd left home, she had run most of the way, refusing to rest and taking poor care of herself. Therefore, returning felt like a long journey because she was injured. Also, since they were heading back from a different path, they were taking all the time in the world, especially since they'd had to stop for a day because Maroon had become sick.

"It's worth it," Maroon said to herself.

"What is worth it?" Slate asked.

"Oh, I, um …" Maroon hadn't realized she had spoken out loud. "This journey. I just think it's worth it if I get to save my friends in the end."

"Yeah," Slate replied. "Being a hero, it's not just saving things. It is standing up for those you care about. I think you are a hero, Maroon, because you risked your life to save your friends from the bears. And when you got sick, you never gave up."

"Th-thank you?" Maroon said, shocked at what she was hearing. She had never been called a hero before. Not even Violet had ever called her something like that, her best friend.

"Maroon? Um, well, we are not still enemies, are we? I mean, I don't like being enemies, and—"

"No," Maroon interrupted him, "we're not enemies anymore. But we're not friends, and we will never be. We can be called partners or something."

"Oh, okay!" Slate seemed less than delighted but was still happy with the decision.

As nightfall approached, Maroon asked Slate about his family and how they were doing, only to have him stalk into the bushes with his tail dragging behind.

What is that about? she thought.

Maroon noticed his bleak behavior and approached the bushes. Crouching in the snow, she listened to Slate's sighs and shuffling. Then he gazed up into the sky with his ears flattened.

"I should have tried to protect you," he whined.

Maroon burst through the leaves, walking up beside him. "What? What are you talking about? Are you talking about leaving my friends? Did they all actually die?" Maroon hollered.

Slate whirled around, startled and distressed at realizing that Maroon had heard him. Then he averted his gaze, upset.

"Oh, it's nothing. I am fine!" Slate spoke firmly.

Maroon snarled, but Slate took no notice.

Maroon huffed. *How does he not even flinch at my threatening behavior? He never acted so uninterested in anything before, so why is he acting like this now?*

"Look, it has nothing to do with you or your friends, so you don't have to worry. It's just ..." Slate sighed and began to pad away. "I just don't want to talk about it."

Maroon followed him, her suspicions of Slate being a traitor slowly returning. *He has secrets*, she began to think. *And I must uncover them.*

***

Maroon spent half the night carefully pushing small branches and rocks to form a wall around where Slate slept. She put more weight on all her legs, except her injured one.

Maroon looked at Slate, his face unreadable in his sleep, but Maroon knew he was hiding something. Then she shook him awake.

Slate curled his tail over his face and mumbled unknown words.

"Not enough, ey?" Maroon spoke to herself then opened her jaws.

"Wake up!" she yelled.

Slate's eyes widened in alarm, and he sprang up, looking wildly from side to side, his chest heaving.

"What?" he managed to speak.

"I know you're hiding something," Maroon said, circling around him, causing him to cower in fear. "I want to know what it is," she demanded.

Slate lowered his bristling fur and flattened his ears in pity. "I told you I didn't want to talk about it. But if hiding it makes me suspicious, I will tell you. It's about my family …"

Chapter Twenty
Slate's Past

H ave you ever heard of the story about the flying fox?" Slate asked.

"Yes," Maroon responded. "All foxes are taught that story when they are young. It's a myth, isn't it? About some winged fox who flew away when his home was destroyed by Fire?"

"Correct." Slate nodded. "Fire starts out small, but if you feed her, she will grow, spreading and eating the forest until all that is left is ash and smoke."

Maroon shut her eyes and shook her head. "It's a terrible thing," she said. "Once a Fire is born, she cannot be stopped. She only stops when she runs out of things to destroy."

Slate sighed. "Fire came to me."

Maroon's eyes widened as she gazed at Slate. "Are you serious?"

"Yes, when I was just old enough to leave my parents." Slate sat down and looked at Maroon then stared at an unseen place. "All I remember is fear and Fire's cackling laugh as she devoured all I knew."

Slate looked so sad that Maroon almost had pity for him.

"Tell me what happened, and you can add details. I know you love telling long stories." Maroon tried to brighten the mood but was awkwardly hushed by Slate's upset glance.

"It was one morning ... Fire only comes when she's angry. I was old enough to leave the den and start my own life, but I was scared. I didn't want to be alone out in the woods, so I told my mother and father how much I would miss them when I left. Then my brothers and I left together. My brothers wanted to start their own adventures, so they went their separate ways and left me alone. Then I remembered wanting to go back home, just to live with my family for a little longer.

"When I returned to the tree—it had a burrow below it—all I remember seeing was the fire. She had trapped my parents inside, surrounding them and keeping me from saving them. The smoke was so hot that when I got close, the fire would scorch my fur, and when I tried to go into the burrow, her flames would grow in front of me, keeping me out and choking me.

"I was so scared I called my brothers back. They returned and went in to save Mother and Father, but I was too afraid to follow them. Then I remember the fire got so mad, and I was forced to run. After that day, I learned never to be afraid to risk my life to save someone. I could have saved my family, but I was a coward." Slate finished his story with a whine, and Maroon felt strong grief wash over her.

Why have I been so mean to him? she thought. *If he's been carrying this burden for so long, am I the first one he's confessed it to?*

"Slate," Maroon started, "I want you to know that I'm sorry for what you had to go through and how I've treated you. You've been very nice to me, and I never should have said some things to you. I'm sorry."

Slate cheered up a little and responded with, "Thank you, Maroon. I don't think I have ever mentioned that you found your gem. Do you know how rare it is for any fox to find their gem? You should be so proud."

"I am, and that's why, if anyone lays a claw on it, I will send them running into the forest, roaring in pain!" Maroon joked, jumping onto her paws. "No one can defeat me!"

"Well, that's because you haven't gone through me first!" Slate laughed and swished his tail in a game.

"I'd like to see you try!" Maroon growled and jumped at Slate. He dodged out of the way and collided into her side. Maroon then kicked and snapped, eventually managing to push Slate off.

She scrambled to her paws and looked from left to right, looking for Slate.

A snap from a branch told her to look up, and when she did, she saw Slate looking at her from over his shoulder, his paws firmly gripping the bark of a tree.

"Cheater!" Maroon called.

"I could teach you how to climb!" Slate suggested as he continued up the tree.

"Fine, but I want to win first!" Maroon barked, pacing around the tree.

Slate suddenly pummeled down from the tree with a screech, landing on top of her.

Maroon felt her legs buckle underneath the weight, and her breath was sucked out of her. Then the weight was gone, and she staggered to her paws, gasping.

"Did I win?" Slate asked, chuckling.

"You wouldn't have if you hadn't climbed a tree!" Maroon grumbled, shaking out her fur. "What was that, anyway?"

"It is a technique in the trees," Slate told her. "Gray foxes often use it in play fights."

"It's rough." Maroon started smoothing down her fur. "But don't think I can't handle it, because I can!"

"Maroon!" Slate sprang up in excitement.

"What? What is it?" Maroon looked around.

"Your leg! You are standing on it!" Slate yelped.

Maroon looked down at her leg, expecting to see red-colored snow. Instead, she noticed the previously split skin was slowly forming together. Maroon had not even felt the pain until Slate had mentioned it.

She felt a new wave of excitement go through her. At this rate, she would be completely healed by the time they returned home. And, if that was the case, she would be ready to take on the wolves!

Chapter Twenty-One
Tree Climbing

T he sun's morning rays warmed Maroon's back. She felt refreshed and confident because she could now walk on her paw without limping as much.

Slate was in a playful mood today, running around and barking, scrambling up a tree, and jumping down in front of her to give chase. Maroon would sometimes join in on the fun, chasing Slate at a careful pace, but she mostly was kept amused at his pup-like behavior. Twice, they stopped for prey, yet they rarely found any water source. Finally, after a while, Slate stopped and sat down. He usually always sat down when he talked.

"So, when would you like to start practicing tree climbing?" he asked.

Maroon stopped and cocked her head. "Oh, right," she spoke. "I forgot I'd agreed to that. Well, um, why not now?"

Slate sprang up and waved his tail. "Great! Come; I'll teach you!" He turned and bounded to the nearest oak tree. "Watch how I climb," he said as he shuffled quickly up the tree.

Snow splashed against her as he landed by her side.

"Your turn," he said.

Maroon turned toward the tree, tail flicking in determination. Then she walked up to the trunk, put a paw uselessly onto the bark, and then her other paw higher up. She tried heaving herself up the tree, struggling to get off the ground.

After a few exhausting attempts to get up the tree, muttering, "Fox gems," under her breath several times, she sank to the ground, panting.

Slate walked up to her and cocked his head. Then he put out his paw and turned it to show the paw pads underneath. He told

Maroon to do the same then looked at both of Maroon's paws and his own paw, comparing them.

Maroon's toes were longer, her claws duller, and her pads firmer. Slate's paw had shorter toes but longer claws. His paws were more cat-like, which explained why he climbed so well.

Maroon put her paw down in annoyance. How was she supposed to climb like Slate when she didn't even have good claws?

She flattened her ears when she heard Slate speak.

"Well, if you can't climb the tree from the ground, maybe you could get higher up in the tree first."

"And, how do you suppose I'll do that?" she snarled.

Slate stood up and walked away from the tree. "Running and jumping, of course!" he finally said, backing up then sprinting toward the oak before jumping at the last second onto a lower branch.

"Because this is an oak, it has low-hanging branches, so you will be able to climb trees similar to this. Aspen or any other tree with high or skinny branches, you won't jump high enough to reach," Slate instructed from the treetops as he climbed higher.

"I think I got the idea without you having to explain it!" Maroon yelled up at the sky. "Can you come down? I don't appreciate having to raise my voice!"

"Sure," Slate said then jumped off the tree. "Here, why don't you try now?" He smiled.

Copying Slate's instructions, she backed away from the tree, eyes focused on the branch she wanted to climb. Then she began to run with a deep breath, snow reeling away under her paws.

"Jump!" Slate called.

The second she heard this cry, she sprang at the tree, landing halfway on the branch.

"Dig your claws in!" Slate exclaimed in worry.

Maroon dug her claws into the branch without hesitation, heaving herself up until her hind legs had a steady grip on the wood.

"Great!" Slate said, climbing up after her. "Stay there on that branch, and I'll come and help you."

Maroon looked around at the following possible places she could climb.

"Okay." Slate was clinging only to the tree's trunk but seemed perfectly calm. Now at the same level as Maroon, he could give her better instructions. "See that branch? Because that is closest and not too high, you want to get on that one next. Then just work your way up the tree," Slate told her, examining her every move as she reached out for the next branch.

Maroon rose slowly onto her hind legs, her paws quaking in fear. Then she hooked her front claws over the next branch and carefully brought herself onto it. The higher she got, the easier it was because of the many branches clustered together.

Slate called out instructions as she climbed and even helped her when she got stuck.

When she reached the highest point on the oak, she was rewarded with an incredible sight. The trees glistened with a white coating of snow, the mountain peaks reached up to the blue sky, and how big and vast the forest was … it stretched beyond sight.

Wow, Maroon thought, amazed. *If this is the world, I'm glad to be a part of it.*

"Maroon! Come look!"

Slate's cry startled her, and she quickly climbed down, branch after branch, until she was on the ground.

"Look!" Slate said, crouching down and pacing around something in excitement.

"What is it, Slate?" Maroon asked, walking toward him.

"It's a weasel," Slate said happily.

Maroon moved closer and saw an animal as large as Slate, brown-furred, with long hairs spread out on all sides except its tiny face. It faced the foxes, eyes wide in alert and its spiked tail swishing in warning.

Maroon growled at the animal, signaling that she would keep the peace as long as it did the same.

"I can hunt it!" Slate growled, approaching the animal.

Maroon grabbed him by the scruff and yanked him back.

He yelped and stumbled into the snow, getting up soon to glare at her. "Why did—"

"That's no weasel," Maroon interrupted. "That's a porcupine. Large, walking prey with hairs sharper than fangs. Their quills aren't just sharp, they're barbed, meaning that once they go in you, they don't come back out."

Slate stared at Maroon with wide eyes then turned his head to stare at the porcupine, who wasn't swishing its tail anymore but kept its eyes locked on the foxes. Then Slate stood up, taking in a big whiff of the porcupine's scent to lock it in his memory.

Maroon growled at the porcupine a second time then led Slate away from that part of the forest and left the porcupine to continue its meal.

Chapter Twenty-Two
Home

Walking steadily, Maroon and Slate again started on the long journey home.

Maroon had forgotten about her promise to never return home. She had a good reason to break that promise, anyway.

Slate had started his poetry once more, using the things he passed as ideas.

Maroon was getting annoyed by the constant word's spilling out of his mouth. She again wished he would be quiet.

"Who did you learn poetry from?" she asked. "Your mother?"

"Well, yes," Slate responded sadly, gazing at his paws.

"I'm sorry, I shouldn't have asked that," she apologized.

"It is okay. I am learning to get over it," Slate told her then paused to sniff the air.

"Look," he whispered. "It's a rabbit! I'll go after it. You are still healing."

"No," Maroon growled. "I know this rabbit." She then approached the rabbit, leaving Slate behind with an open mouth.

She cocked her head when she saw the rabbit and stopped in front of it.

It stayed put, perfectly calm.

"I remember you," Maroon told the rabbit. "You helped me when I was in the trap. Thank you."

"Wait—a rabbit *helped* you?" Slate exclaimed.

"Be quiet. I'm in the middle of talking with someone!" Maroon snapped at him then turned back toward the rabbit.

The rabbit nodded as if she understood everything Maroon had said. Then, with her mouth, the rabbit picked up something sitting behind her.

Maroon cocked her head again, curious at what the rabbit was holding. Looking into the green plant, Maroon recognized it as a clover.

"Are you giving us food?" Maroon asked the rabbit, who shook her head and set the clover down, putting her tiny paw on it.

"Clover! That must be her name," Slate told Maroon.

Suddenly, the rabbit nodded, and Maroon realized he was right.

"Your name is Clover?" Maroon inquired.

Clover nodded again.

"Hello, Clover," Slate said kindly, approaching the rabbit. "How are you?"

Clover twitched her nose then turned to Maroon.

"Don't bother her," Maroon told Slate. "Besides, she can't talk to us."

"Then how does she know what we are saying?" Slate asked.

"She can understand us, but she cannot speak back as a prey animal," Maroon snapped at him in annoyance. Then they both stared at each other in silence. The only sound was the wind in the trees. Maroon spoke first, needing to say something.

"Slate, this journey with you has been unexpected in so many ways. You've told me about yourself, and I'd like to hear more. You've tried your best to solve any problem we've faced, and you helped me recover from being sick. I want to thank you. More importantly, I want to put our rivalry aside for good."

Slate was shocked to silence then smiled.

Maroon held out her paw and looked at Slate. "Friends?" she asked.

Slate's smile grew even broader, and he put his paw to hers. "Friends," he finished.

A happy squeak came from behind them, and Marron turned to see Clover hopping around in joy. She then noticed how the forest looked livelier and more welcoming than it had on her whole journey.

I guess living in a world and hating someone only made me the one I hated, Maroon told herself. *Well, I'm glad I finally let go of it.*

Maroon turned to Clover. "I noticed you only show up when something is going on. Do you have something to show me?"

Clover nodded then bounded away, leaving small prints in the snow to follow.

Maroon flicked her tail. "Come on, Slate; let's go."

The two friends ran side by side, paws pounding the earth below. Slate started rasping, and Maroon felt her gem begin to bounce.

Following Clover with a new friend by her side, she felt something that had stayed away for too long—happiness.

The trees looked familiar as Maroon ran. Soon after, she could hear the trickle of a stream.

My stream! was the only thought she had as she ran on.

Bursting through the bushes, she saw her log coated with snow and welcoming her home. Yelping in delight, Maroon ran to the water's edge, smashing a paw down to break the ice. She drank. She was home.

"It is nice to be back." A voice sounded from behind as Slate approached her.

Maroon smiled and turned to Clover. "Thank you."

With a nod, Clover turned and hopped away.

Looking down at her paw, Maroon saw it was fully healed, with a mark left behind as a scar, for which she was proud.

Maroon lifted her head and breathed in the beautiful scent of home. She smelled the trees and the smell of nearby burrows, but then she suddenly smelled the powerful odor of a wolf.

Her eyes widened in fear. She had forgotten about the wolves.

She dove through the thorn bushes and into her log with a yelp, terrified of being found.

Slate crept in after her, also trembling.

"What do we do now?" Maroon asked, afraid that a wolf patrol would show up at any moment.

Slate thought for a moment then said, "Well, let's not run in and save anyone for now. Instead, let's find and meet up with anyone that escaped before the wolves started enforcing their territory. If we can find them, we can all come up with a plan to save the others. Also, the wolves did not take over your log. Where we are right now is just on the border of their territory. We might find some others if we can sneak around their border to the coyote territory. Then maybe we can stop the wolves."

Chapter Twenty-Three
Finding Familiar Faces

Maroon and Slate stopped to look around. Finally, they had made it to the coyote territory. Maroon remembered this place as the place she had met Thrash.

As far from the wolf territory as possible, Maroon looked to Slate and said, "You said they would be here!"

Slate nodded. "I know, but we have to look for them first." Then he bent his head to sniff the ground and flicked his tail for Maroon to do the same.

Maroon ignored him and raised her head to catch scents wafting through the air. What seemed like hours of searching, she noticed a smell. It was fresh, and it had a pup odor present.

With a bark, Maroon raced off as fast as she could in the direction where she had smelled the odor. The sound of panting told her Slate was behind her.

Stopping to sniff for more clues, she saw a bundle of fur lying in the snow. At first, Maroon thought it was a wolf, but then she remembered they were not in wolf territory.

Slate gasped and ran over to the animal. Maroon followed, ears forward in alert.

The orange pelt and white-tipped tail told her this animal was a fox, but she did not know who from the strong scent of blood.

The fox then raised its head, and Maroon was shocked to see that it was Aqua. She was even more surprised to see deep wounds and cuts covering her whole body and jutting bones.

"Aqua!" Maroon cried. "What happened?"

Aqua smiled. "It's nice to see you, Maroon," she spoke as Maroon began licking the blood from her wounds.

"Tell me what happened," Maroon demanded, more of an order than a question.

Aqua's happiness faded, and she forced back a moan of pain. "The wolves did this."

Before she could continue, Maroon let out a growl.

"I had it worse out of everyone else because I was defending my kits, but I couldn't die and leave them motherless. So, I had to run away." She paused to flinch in pain. "Luckily, they are safe in the den, but they are trapped until the wolves are gone for good."

Maroon paced back and forth in rage, and Slate took Maroon's place in licking Aqua's wounds.

Finally, Maroon said, "Where's your mate?"

"Bronze?" Aqua responded. "He didn't make it out."

"You mean the wolves killed him?" Maroon growled.

"I'm not sure," Aqua responded. "But I know the wolves are taking hostages, and Violet is one of them."

Maroon yelped in surprise. Violet, her best friend, had been taken hostage. How terrible.

She would love to tear those forest dogs apart.

Maroon heard the sounds of approaching paw steps from behind. She turned to see Mahogany coming toward them, holding a strip of bark with moss on it. When she caught sight of Maroon, she dropped the bark and ran over.

"Maroon!" she barked. "I'm so glad you're back!" She stopped herself, turned around, grabbed the moss, and pressed it to Aqua's wounds.

"Oh, it looks like you've found your gem!" she barked again.

Maroon was impressed by how quickly Mahogany had noticed her gem. She raised her head even higher. Then she saw bite marks and scratches across Mahogany's back, but it seemed almost healed. That caused a question to stir in her mind.

Maroon opened her mouth to ask, "If the journey back home took several days, how come Aqua looks as if she just got those injuries when you look like yours have healed?"

Mahogany stopped and answered, "That's because, after the wolves took over, which was several days after you left, Aqua had to go back in to try to save her pups by the time you were returning."

Maroon gave Aqua a stern look. "Let's not go into wolf territory until we develop a plan."

Aqua began pawing the ground in frustration, and Maroon understood why.

It must be difficult to leave your mate and pups in enemy territory, no matter how injured you've become.

"Where's Thrash?" Maroon asked.

Mahogany and Aqua looked at each other, and then at Maroon.

"He left days ago," Mahogany responded. "A couple of days after you, actually. He must have gone looking for you."

"You mean, he left when I told him not to? He was supposed to protect you!" Maroon swished her tail in rage. Then she stopped when she saw Slate glaring at her, realizing the threat was no longer a problem. "I mean, he was supposed to keep you all company ..." she corrected.

Maroon felt a wave of embarrassment when she saw her friends didn't believe her. They all knew the real reason why Thrash had remained—as a guard.

"Look," Maroon began, "I was wrong. I thought Slate was a traitor, and I should have listened to you." She stopped herself. She wanted to say more, but she decided now was not the right time.

"So," Maroon started again, "how far did Thrash go?"

"I followed his trail a little," Mahogany said. "But that was days ago. He's probably long gone by now."

Maroon frowned. "Thanks a lot, Thrash."

Slate rested his tail on her back to cheer her up. "It won't be that bad," he spoke. "We will still save our friends."

Maroon sighed. "Maybe Thrash is already returning. Maybe he followed our trail all the way back here. Maybe I can wait for him if he's coming back."

Slate cocked his head. "What if he is not coming back?"

"Then we'll forget about him." Maroon smirked and started again on the cautious journey around the wolf territory to get to the stream. Once there, she would follow Thrash's trail and hope he was already back home.

***

Maroon knew why she hadn't run into Thrash on the journey home with Slate. They had taken a different route home, she remembered. So, if Thrash was looking for Maroon, he might be ages away.

Maroon picked her way carefully over the leaf litter and deep piles of snow. She noticed the snow was beginning to melt just a little.

Maroon growled. *So, I spent half the winter walking to a place just to go back with my former enemy when I could have spent it with my friends!*

She sighed. *The sooner I find Thrash, the better. Hopefully, I don't have to go on another long journey just to do so.*

She had been looking for about an hour when she heard the crunch of snow and smelled the musky scent of a coyote.

"Thrash?" Maroon called out.

He emerged from the bushes.

"Thrash!" Maroon barked and ran over to him. She had missed her friend and was glad to see he was his usual self.

"Maroon!" Thrash said, gently wagging his tail. "I was looking for you!"

Then the crunch of snow started again, and Maroon saw someone else emerge beside Thrash.

Maroon looked down at the small yet wise creature. "Kitsune?"

Kitsune dipped his head in respect. "Glad to see you made it out of the trap."

Thrash looked alarmed. "Trap? You never told me she got caught in a trap!"

Kitsune grinned. "That's because you didn't need to know. Since she's perfectly fine, you wouldn't have known at all."

Thrash nodded, averted his gaze in shame, and Maroon grinned in amusement.

"So," Maroon started to ask with curiosity, "how did you two meet?"

Thrash opened his jaws to reply, but Kitsune interrupted him with a smirk. "After I led the dogs away from you, I ran into my shed and out of the emergency escape I had dug. It was too small for any large, blundering dog to fit through; they were confused. Then, when they left, I went over to your burrow so they wouldn't know where I had gone."

Thrash looked even more alarmed than before.

"You never told me you had an emergency escape," Maroon accused.

Kitsune shrugged. "Why do I need to tell you when it was my secret?"

Thrash stepped forward, shocked after hearing about the dogs. "Anyway, I followed your trail to a burrow dangerously located in the territory of a trapper's cabin." He glared at Maroon, and she snarled back in defense. "It was there where I met Kitsune, and he told me you returned home. I do not know how he knew that, but he and I followed your scent back here." Thrash seemed delighted. "So, I guess we can all go back home?"

"Not so fast." Maroon stopped them both in their tracks.

Kitsune stopped to scratch his ear as if Maroon wasn't even there.

Maroon looked at the territory that had once belonged to them then looked back at Thrash and Kitsune. "A wolf pack took over."

Chapter Twenty-Four
Wolf Territory

I'm still surprised you went all the way to the trapper's cabin!" Maroon exclaimed, impressed that Thrash had gone on the same long journey that she had taken.

Maroon and Thrash were sitting together in Thrash's old territory, a place the wolf pack hadn't claimed. The rest of her friends were also there; some hunting for prey, others resting in the shade.

"I'm sorry about leaving," Thrash told her. "I should have listened to you and stayed home. If only I had known a wolf pack was the real danger instead of Slate. I'm sorry." He licked her ear in an apology, and Maroon expressed forgiveness.

Just then, Kitsune came up to them, barking. "I need an aloe vera plant. It's the ultimate healer of wounds!"

Maroon shook her head, thinking he was making stuff up, but the plant could have only been in Africa. "I've never even heard of an aloe vera."

When Kitsune began to describe what it looked like, Maroon shook her head again. "Never heard of it."

Kitsune growled. "Don't you foxes have anything here?" At that, he spun around and scampered away.

Maroon got up. "I'm going to go calm him down. He's never acted like this before."

Thrash shrugged. "Well, he must hate wounds. When I got a scratch, he did the same thing."

Maroon let out a bark in amusement. "That must be his weakness then."

She began walking toward Kitsune, but then she veered in the direction of wolf territory when Thrash wasn't looking.

I want to save my friends, and I'll do that in any way possible, she thought.

When she had come to the border of the wolf territory, she stopped, sniffing and beginning to pace back and forth, desperate to get in, but the scent marks said. "Warning."

Maroon set one paw over the territory's border, and then another. Soon, she was entirely on the wolves' ground.

"This was ours first," she said to herself as she walked through the familiar forest.

When she heard a rustle in the bushes behind her, she turned to face it with snarling teeth. She reminded herself that she was still on wolf territory when no other sound came from the bushes.

Maroon felt her fur rising along her spine as she walked deeper into the forest. Finally, she came across Slate's abandoned burrow and decided to crawl inside. She'd hated Slate so much that she had never even thought of going anywhere near his burrow, but now that they were friends, she couldn't help herself.

The tunnel entrance was narrow, but it opened up as she made it to the den area. Maroon saw the burrow walls and a nest made from leaves in the center. Studying it, she wondered if the bedding was really that comfortable. But, of course, she wouldn't know because she always slept on solid ground, even in her log.

Then she noticed another tunnel further back. Crawling over Slate's nest, she squeezed through it and back out into the forest, except she had come out a different way than the way she had gone in.

Does Slate really have two entrances? she thought to herself. *Why would he worry about two ways to get in?*

Maroon turned away from the burrow and deeper into wolf territory. She hadn't walked much further when she halted at the nearby wolf scent.

Maroon turned and stalked into the bushes, peering out from behind.

She was near Violet's burrow, not too far from the stream. As she crept closer, she could even see Violet's den—a crack in some large rocks—and sitting next to it, she could make out the two distinct shapes of wolves.

They were both guarding the entrance, and Maroon guessed that was where they were keeping Violet, Magenta, and Bronze. Maybe even the pups.

Maroon pricked her ears at the sound of voices. She turned and crept through the bushes enough to see where it was coming from. There, she saw two other wolves—a black wolf with gray eyes and a gray wolf with yellow eyes. They were speaking to each other in a severe tone.

"I'm telling you, Shadow, foxes live right outside our territory. They could be trouble," the gray wolf said to the wolf named Shadow.

"I know, Fang," Shadow spoke. "Those weak little foxes think they can swoop in and take what's ours. Don't worry; we can ask Alpha to send out some wolves to keep watch. Those pesky animals would have to be stupid enough to think they could come into our territory. They must have some sort of death wish." The wolf named Shadow chuckled and glanced over at Violet's den with a smirk.

Maroon couldn't help but let out a tiny growl. *Those wolves think they can mock us like that, and now I'm positive that Violet's den is where they're keeping my friends.*

Fang glanced at the den then back at Shadow. "I don't know. We did capture some of their family. They must really want them back if they haven't left by now. We should probably just give their family back, and they will all go far away."

Shadow's smile disappeared, and his gray eyes flashed in anger. "Do you really want foxes to think of us all as allies if we kindly give their friends back? Of course, if they come into our territory, we can just rip them apart. But we aren't letting those foxes go if it makes us look weak."

Fang looked at the ground then up at Shadow. "Of course. I was just about to say that."

Shadow rolled his eyes then got up. "Now, if you will excuse me," he spoke. "I have to get back to my pup."

Maroon raised her tail in alert. *They have pups? If I can maybe steal one, we could make a deal with the wolves. If they release my friends, I'll give their pups back.*

She grinned. *Now, where do I find one?*

She looked around, but the more she did, the more she realized how many wolves there were. Finally, not seeing a single wolf pup, Maroon turned and started heading back in the direction of the coyote territory. She stopped to hide behind a bush as a patrol of wolves walked past. She was lucky that she smelled enough like a wolf for them not to find her.

After she had passed Slate's burrow again, she enjoyed the breeze when she felt something pounce on her tail.

With a yelp, Maroon spun around, only to see a wolf pup giggling in amusement. It was white and gray in color, with one solid black paw and a black stripe up its muzzle. It had the same looking face as the wolf called Shadow.

This must be his pup, Maroon thought as she gazed at the creature.

It rolled around in delight then sat up to say, "Got you!"

Maroon stared at the wolf pup in annoyance. *This pup clearly has no idea how dangerous it is to go near other predators. It even left the den all by itself!* Maroon thought.

"What's your name?" Maroon asked the pup.

"Needle!" the pup responded, clearly a female. Then she gazed at Maroon. "Wow, your fur is so pretty. And, is that a purple rock? Can I have it?"

Maroon growled at the pup. The last thing she would ever do was hand away her gem to some random stranger.

Needle got up and ran around Maroon, laughing.

Maroon growled again, louder this time. "Stop that! What are you doing here?"

"I just wanted to meet you. Your fur is so pretty," Needle said.

Maroon grumbled then spoke. "What is your pack up to?"

"Oh, nothing much. They just said they would ambush some foxes." Needle scratched her ear.

"Ambush?" Maroon replied in horror.

"Yeah, you know, pretend to abandon the territory, and then the nasty foxes come in and *surprise!* they all die!"

Maroon gasped then looked at the wolf pup, who was staring at her gem. "Do you even know what a fox is?"

Needle looked at Maroon, paying no attention to how different in size Maroon would be from a wolf. "My father says foxes are big, nasty creatures that hunt at night and slay as many pups as the stars in the sky. They have blood-red fur and eyes." She shivered at the thought.

Maroon flattened her ears. "You know I'm a fox, right?"

"Oh ... sorry," Needle said, lowering her head in shame, somehow not terrified of how vicious she had just explained foxes were.

Maroon grinned. "To us foxes, wolves are the scary ones."

Needle perked up her ears. "Really?"

Maroon nodded.

"That's so cool! I didn't know foxes had such pretty fur." Needle looked at Maroon. "Or that they don't seem nasty at all."

Maroon rolled her eyes. *This wolf won't stop talking about my fur, but I think my plan will work with this pup.*

"Hey, Needle, would you like to meet other pretty foxes?" Maroon asked.

Needle looked up in excitement, "There are more of you?"

Maroon nodded and grinned. "Yes, and if you want to meet them ... follow me."

Chapter Twenty-Five
Stealing Needle

Needle ran ahead through the snow, laughing and gazing at every "pretty" thing she saw.

While she was distracted, Maroon mumbled to herself, "This is perfect. Once the wolves find out that I've captured Needle, they'll be forced to release my friends. But if they think they can come over and take her themselves, I won't think twice if I have to hurt her. I will do anything for my friends."

As they walked on, Needle paused to look at a pine cone. "I found another to add to my collection!" she exclaimed proudly.

"You like to collect things?" Maroon asked.

Needle nodded. "Yeah, but I love pine cones; they're so pretty!"

Maroon sighed, wondering if that was the sixth or the seventh time Needle had said "pretty."

"I have a friend who also collects things," Maroon told her.

Needle looked excited. "Really? I can't wait to go meet them! I used to have a huge pine cone collection, but my mother threw it out and said I should stop wasting my time with filth."

Maroon was shocked. *Does her family even care about Needle, or are they just trying to make her as cruel-hearted as themselves?*

"Do you have any food? I'm starving!" Needle said, looking directly at Maroon's mouth.

Maroon started, "Can't you see that I'm not carrying anything?" Then she realized that canines usually store extra food in their stomachs for pups, but only when they are too young to eat big chunks of meat.

"Aren't you a little old to be eating regurgitated food?" Maroon asked.

Needle bounced as they walked. "Yes, but when there is no food nearby, I will eat the food my parents stored for me."

Maroon grumbled. Was she really going to give this pup the food in her stomach? She didn't even want to, and she was not about to force herself into doing something that she did not want to do.

"Can't you wait until I find some prey that we could both share?" Maroon asked.

"Fine," Needle said, keeping her eyes on the ground the rest of the way.

**

They kept walking until Maroon could see the end of the trees in the distance and the start of coyote territory.

"I'm so bored!" Needle exclaimed, moaning and kicking the snow as she walked.

Maroon growled, "We're almost there." She didn't want to alert any wolves that they were there, but after she'd said that, she heard a deep bark, and then five big wolves ran up to her and Needle, surrounding them.

One had a sand-colored pelt with orange eyes. One had a gray pelt with green eyes, and two others were white and gray. The last one was light brown. They all had torn ears and scars on their bodies. Some even had scars on one of their front legs.

The wolves growled and snapped at Maroon, ears flat in distress. They all looked big and strong.

"Just where do you think you were going, fox?" the sand-colored wolf spoke, coughing out "fox" in disgust.

Maroon snarled and brought Needle closer to her. "I was just leaving."

"Leaving?" the sand-colored wolf spoke again. "With a pup?"

Maroon growled even louder and dug her claws into the snow.

"We should just kill her, Steel!" a gray wolf shouted. "If she's stealing pups, she must be taught a lesson."

The tan wolf named Steel glared at the wolf who spoke to silence him.

"Stealing pups, are we?" Steel asked.

Maroon shook her head, annoyed by how the wolf spoke to her.

"Then where are you taking Needle?" Steel snapped.

Maroon swallowed and looked at Needle, who was wagging her tail in delight at seeing the other wolves.

Of course, she's not afraid, Maroon thought. *This is her family pack.*

Maroon replied, "Well, I found this pup wandering alone, so I thought I would bring her back."

For a second, the wolves were unsure how to respond to that. Steel was staring at Maroon, and she noticed a hint of concern in his eyes.

Maroon was grinning now. *I have their pup; they should be concerned.*

Steel flicked his tail in a signal to bring another wolf toward him.

"Check the paw prints," Steel told the wolf, who nodded and trotted off in the direction she had come.

Maroon froze. *Oh no,* she thought. *If they check my paw prints and see that I wasn't bringing Needle back, I'm doomed!*

When Steel saw the fear in Maroon's eyes, it was his turn to grin in satisfaction.

The other wolf returned to Steel's side and said something in Steel's ear. Steel nodded with a nasty look on his face.

"So, where were you taking her?" Steel growled with a smile.

Maroon swallowed, terrified of what might happen if she answered wrong, not that they needed an answer anymore.

"Thorn, take Needle back home. I've got some work to do," Steel spoke, his eyes locked on Maroon.

A brown wolf stepped out of the group and called Needle over.

Needle ran excitedly past Maroon and followed the brown wolf without a second thought.

Maroon sighed. Her plan had failed, and Needle seemed to have forgotten about the rivalry between wolves and foxes. Did Needle even care about what would happen to her?

Steel's low voice interrupted her thoughts.

"We should take you to Alpha. I bet he would love to hear about where you were taking Needle."

Some other wolves nodded in agreement.

Maroon couldn't help but shrink back. She wished she was back with Aqua and her other friends instead of in wolf territory.

As the circle closed in, Maroon could see the fangs of bloodthirsty wolves and the gleam of ferociousness in their eyes.

Maroon closed her eyes and let them inch closer. Then, with an explosion of wind and buzzing, Maroon could no longer feel the wolves' hot breath on her pelt. Instead, she heard the yelps of wolves in pain and felt a few stings of pain herself.

She opened her eyes to see a flurry of wasps in an angry swarm, attacking the wolves with their stingers. Maroon ducked behind a bush before they could sting her again.

Looking out from around the bush, she saw a crushed and split open wasp hive on the snow where the wasps must have come out.

Did it fall from a tree? she thought.

Before she could react, she felt teeth secure around her scruff, and then she was thrown back.

She looked up to see Mahogany with wide eyes.

She pushed Maroon to her paws and said, "We have to run. Hurry!"

Chapter Twenty-Six
The Betrayal

So, you were hiding behind the bush that whole time?" Maroon spoke as she ran with Mahogany directly beside her.

"Yes," Mahogany answered. "I was holding a stick with a small wasp hive and tossed it as soon as I saw you in trouble."

"But you saw me when I first met Needle?" Maroon asked, panting. "And when I first went into wolf territory?"

Mahogany nodded.

"But you didn't do anything!" Maroon was yelling now.

"You didn't seem to need help, except when the wolf patrol caught you. Besides, you hate it when someone helps you," Mahogany responded before she ran ahead.

Maroon flattened her ears, annoyed that Mahogany was right.

When the two foxes made it back to coyote territory, Thrash ran up to them, looking anxious.

"Where were you two? I was so worried about you!" Thrash demanded, lashing his tail.

Maroon spoke, "Calm down. We were just—"

"Scouting!" Mahogany interrupted her.

Thrash flattened his ears and glared at them. "Where?"

"Over by the wolf territory," Maroon answered, knowing that if she told half the truth, Thrash would believe her.

"We didn't go in. We just looked for weak points in their border," Mahogany concluded.

Thrash stood frozen, staring at the two with unblinking eyes. His ear twitched, and he sighed. "Fine, but don't go into their territory again, and don't think I didn't see you."

Maroon grinned and flicked her tail in pleasure. Then she padded past Thrash with Mahogany trailing behind.

***

"Did you see my pups?" Aqua asked, clearly worried.

"No," Maroon responded. She then proceeded to tell Aqua about her sneaking into wolf territory, and she did not leave out a single detail. "But I know the wolves are planning an ambush—Needle told me."

"How can you trust her? She's a wolf. She could have been lying," Aqua replied.

"She's a wolf *pup*," Maroon answered. "Besides, I'm thinking of kidnapping her so the wolves will give back our friends."

Maroon looked behind her at the sound of paw steps.

Slate was running up to her with an excited look on his face. Beside him was Kitsune, who was ambling along.

"Kitsune has a plan!" Slate exclaimed, wagging his tail. "It will help us with the wolves!"

Maroon perked up her ears in interest. *Will it save my friends?* she thought.

Kitsune sat down, flattening the snow around him to get comfortable.

Maroon flattened her ears in annoyance by how long it took the elder to speak.

"All we need to do is go over and talk to them," he explained.

"What!" Maroon gasped. "They'll kill us!"

"Not if we come in peace," Kitsune continued. "The best way to get your friends back is to ally with the wolves."

"You want to make friends with wolves?" Maroon choked out the words. "They will never trust us."

"Perhaps they will trust me," Kitsune said, walking away.

Maroon stared after him blankly.

***

121

Maroon walked behind Kitsune, with Mahogany and Slate following. They had both come along in case something happened, while Thrash stayed behind to look after Aqua. Kitsune was taking them to talk with the wolf pack, even though Maroon knew this would not get them anywhere.

As they continued walking through the snow, getting wetter as spring was on the way, Maroon stopped when she smelled wolves nearby.

"I think there are some wolves not too far away," Slate said in unease. They were right on the border of wolf territory, waiting patiently for a patrol to spot them.

Kitsune glared at him to silence him, and Slate pawed at the snow.

Magenta looked around for any shiny objects and continuously asked Maroon where she had found her gem.

Soon enough, they heard loud growls and paw steps. Then four large, broad-shouldered wolves stepped out and faced the foxes, snarling.

Maroon recognized Steel in the lead. His sand-colored pelt had several red, swollen bumps, all stings from the wasps. Maroon noticed these were all the same wolves from her last encounter, and all of them had red wasp stings. The only wolf that was not there was the brown wolf called Thorn, probably looking after Needle instead of patrolling with the others.

"Stop! What are you pests doing here?" Steel shouted. "This is wolf territory now. Get over it!"

Several of the other wolves nodded in agreement, all growling.

Maroon growled back, unafraid.

In response, a gray wolf gave her a hard stare, in which Maroon stared back.

Then Kitsune spoke. "We aren't here to fight. We would like to make a deal."

Steel darted his gaze from fox to fox, looking for the one who had spoken. When his eyes came to Kitsune, he stopped snarling and raised his ears.

"Kitsune!" he exclaimed. "Is that you?"

Maroon stood shocked. *How does he know his name? Are they friends?* she worried.

Kitsune smiled. "Nice to see you again, Steel, after the trapper's cabin."

"I know, it was terrible. I'm glad you helped us out, though," Steel responded.

Maroon stared. Had Kitsune helped out more animals than she had thought? *Did the trapper get one of the wolves? How much is Kitsune hiding?*

"So, how about you join us, Kitsune? Alpha would love to have you, and everyone would welcome you," Steel told him.

Kitsune flicked his ears, thinking.

He wouldn't betray us, Maroon thought. *He's our friend.*

"First, I would like you to know that these are my friends." Kitsune waved his tail at the other foxes. "And I would like you to leave them in peace."

Steel sighed and flattened his ears. "We will only leave them in peace if they do the same to us."

"Then it's settled." Kitsune stood up, nodded politely to the wolves, and then turned away.

"Wait!" Steel called, causing Kitsune to look back. "You would have a home here. You'd be happier with us than those rabid foxes! Think of the advantages of living with us! Alpha misses you."

Kitsune thought for a moment, eyes darting from fox to wolf.

"Be wise, Kitsune!" Maroon growled. "Don't listen to them."

Kitsune was about to turn around and rejoin Maroon when he stopped, thinking hard. Then he finally turned to face her. "I'm sorry, Maroon, but he has a point. I've known them longer." That said, to Maroon's horror, he stepped away from her and crossed over the border of wolf territory.

Steel grinned. "Good choice."

Steel and the rest of the patrol, along with Kitsune, headed toward their camp.

"Traitor!" Maroon shouted. Anger and disbelief boiling inside her, she ran right up to the territory's border, snarling and raking her claws through the snow.

Slate and Mahogany stood still, also shocked.

Through the trees, Kitsune looked back at her with emotion in his eyes that she couldn't read.

Maroon stared after him, hate overwhelming her. *Those you used to trust can betray you.*

Mahogany and Slate helped her back to their temporary home while Maroon growled the whole way.

Chapter Twenty-Seven
Planning

Maroon trudged through the snow angrily, snarling with hate at what had happened earlier.

How could Kitsune join them? He betrayed me! He betrayed us! How will he feel if he has to attack us?

In rage, Maroon let out a loud yowl that caused Slate to spring back in fear.

"Calm down," he told her. "He made his choice, and it was not wise, but he could persuade the wolves to free the others."

Maroon rolled her eyes. Slate never seemed to help.

When they returned to camp, Thrash noticed Maroon storming through the snow and quickly stood up. Racing toward the group, he stopped in front of them.

"What happened?" he asked. "Where's Kitsune?"

All three foxes lowered their heads while Maroon growled. Finally, Slate spoke up.

"He left."

"Left? Left to where?" Thrash demanded, putting his face so close to Slate's that Maroon had to shove Thrash away.

In return, Maroon received a grateful look from Slate.

"He joined the wolf pack!" Maroon spat out.

Thrash stood erect, shock pulsing through his entire body. "No, that can't be right! He was my friend. He would never do that!" he exclaimed.

"He was my friend, too!" Maroon told him, sulking as she walked past.

"I'm going hunting," she called out. "Who wants to come with me?"

***

Maroon took another bite of the shrew after Slate and her had brought back enough prey for everyone to share.

Mahogany checked on Aqua, who was slowly getting stronger after being attacked. She refused to eat, still upset about losing her pups and her mate to the wolves.

Maroon growled. She was going to get back all her friends and Aqua's pups, no matter what it took.

"I have a plan!" Thrash announced, causing Maroon to raise her ears in surprise at hearing Thrash speak.

Maroon jumped up. "Will it—"

"Save our friends?" Thrash interrupted. "Yes, it will."

Maroon grinned in delight and barked to get everyone's attention.

"Tell us the plan," Slate demanded, padding up to sit next to Maroon.

Thrash waited as everyone gathered around him. Then he turned around and leaped on top of a boulder so everyone could see him clearly.

Aqua lay licking her wounds, and Mahogany sat beside her.

Behind Thrash, Maroon noticed the sun was beginning to set. *Whatever this plan is*, Maroon thought, *it will have to take place at night.*

"I have tried my best to come up with a plan," Thrash announced, "without Kitsune's help. Though, I am sure he will eventually regret his decision and return to us."

Aqua rolled her eyes in doubt, while Mahogany lowered her gaze.

Maroon snarled, "Kitsune never should have left."

Thrash paced on the boulder, waving his tail in determination. "This plan will need all of you." His gaze then rested on Aqua. "You can stay because you are in no condition to run."

Aqua groaned, probably upset to be left out in the attempt to get her pups back.

"Maroon and Mahogany," Thrash spoke, looking at the two, "you two will sneak in and free the hostages. Meanwhile, Slate and I will cause a distraction."

Slate's eyes widened, clearly nervous about the idea.

"Maroon." Thrash's eyes fell on her. "When you went into the wolf territory, did you see where they kept our friends?"

Maroon nodded and stood up. "There are two guards at the entrance to Violet's den. I am sure that's where our friends are."

Thrash nodded in approval. "If Violet's burrow is close to the stream, Slate and I will target the territory by Magenta's den, farthest away from the stream. That should bring most of the wolves there, leaving you and Mahogany enough time to get in and out."

Maroon nodded. This was her chance to get her friends again.

"What if not all wolves go over to the distraction, especially the two guards?" Mahogany spoke out.

Thrash thought for a while then said, "Then you will have to make your own distraction."

Mahogany sat down, annoyed by the unhelpful answer.

Slate pawed at a bare patch of snow in front of him. "When do we start?"

"Now," Thrash spoke, leaping down from the boulder and walking ahead. "Remember the plan."

Maroon felt excitement surge through her fur like electricity as she got up and followed Thrash. Mahogany nuzzled Aqua goodbye, promising she would return soon with her pups. Slate ran to catch up with Maroon, and they headed toward wolf territory.

Chapter Twenty-Eight
The Rescue Mission

Maroon's pelt prickled in anticipation. She was crouched beside Mahogany, fur bristling, waiting for the distraction. They were both a little inside wolf territory, resting by the thorn bushes of Maroon's territory. Because the wolves still hadn't claimed her domain, they had decided to stay there until Thrash and Slate's distraction started. Then they would dash in and free whoever they could.

Maroon thought she should be able to hear the distraction from here if it was at Magenta's den. Sure enough, Maroon listened to the wails of a coyote, followed by Slate's cries. She waited.

Next, she heard the aggressive snarls from the wolves and guessed they were all on their way to attack what had made the sounds. So, with a flick of her tail, she and Mahogany sprang up from their hiding place and ran toward the bramble bush wall.

Maroon ran through it with ease, as she had done many times before. She turned around to see Mahogany grunting, halfway out of the bush. Maroon rolled her eyes and ran back to her, fastening her teeth around her scruff. Maroon pulled, and Mahogany came out of the brush with a loud *snap*.

Both foxes froze, hoping no one had heard the stick break. When the coast was clear, Maroon got up and ran to the nearest bush, signaling for Mahogany to follow.

"We need to be quick about this!" Mahogany breathed. "Those wolves are smart; they'll figure out about the distraction soon enough!"

Maroon nodded. She was sure there were no more wolves in the camp, anyway.

With Mahogany close behind, Maroon sprinted through the forest toward Violet's burrow. They then slowed to a stop, listening for the wolves. Maroon heard lots of barks and growls. She guessed that the wolves had to be chasing Thrash and Slate.

I hope they both are holding up okay, Maroon thought. *The wolves shouldn't catch up with them, but if they give up on the chase, they could start coming back to camp.* She shivered. Maroon knew the wolves wouldn't hesitate to kill them.

Now she was worried, remembering how Slate couldn't run far before collapsing. She whined. She didn't want Slate to die. There was something about how kind he was, how he had never given up on her. He meant something to her.

"Great fox gems!" Mahogany interrupted her thoughts. "Come on; we have to move!"

Maroon shook her fur, and then they both bounded through the trees, slowing down as they neared the wolf camp.

The snow under their paws felt cold as they stopped to crouch behind a bush, looking out for any wolf. Then she heard a yelp in the distance, which sounded familiar.

Slate!

She held her breath as fear ran through her bones, realizing the wolves might have killed him. She closed her eyes. *No, not my friend!*

With a nudge from Mahogany, Maroon looked at her.

"We need to get closer to Violet's den!" she told Maroon.

When Maroon looked into Mahogany's eyes, she saw that Mahogany also feared for Slate.

I hope he's still alive, Maroon thought.

Leaving that thought behind, she got up, and they crept through the bushes, hoping the snow wouldn't crunch beneath them. They both stopped and peered through the bushes.

Spotting Violet's den, Maroon let out a gasp of horror.

Two wolves were still sitting there. The guards had not left when they'd heard the distraction.

It makes sense, Maroon thought. *If every single wolf left, who would ensure the hostages didn't get away?*

Maroon narrowed her eyes in annoyance. *What now?* She could feel Mahogany beside her and guessed she was also troubled about the two wolves.

She heard another howl from the far-off wolves, and then Thrash's voice rang out in the distance.

"What have you done?"

Shocked, Maroon thought, *Slate must have been killed!* She intensely wished she had been the one out there leading the wolves away rather than out here rescuing her friends.

I should have told Thrash, she said to herself. *I should have told him about Slate's weakness, his lack of endurance. It's all my fault!*

But Maroon knew she needed to rescue her friends, to not have his death be in vain.

"How are we going to get rid of these wolves?" Mahogany growled quietly.

"Thrash ..." Maroon spoke.

Mahogany glanced at her in confusion.

"Thrash told us! Create our own distraction," Maroon said, looking for a rock or a stick.

Mahogany sighed but looked around, as well.

Maroon picked up a small rock and hid behind the bush. Then, holding the stone in her mouth, she tossed it into some far away bushes.

The guards pricked up their ears but stayed put, listening.

Mahogany found a stick and also threw it. It landed by the same bushes.

Maroon's fur prickled with unease as she watched the two guards spring up. Their tails lashing and growls rumbling in their throats.

"Show yourselves!" a wolf spoke as they both crept into the bushes.

"Now," Mahogany whispered, crawling out of the bush and making her way over to Violet's den.

Maroon followed.

When they reached the hole in the two small boulders, Maroon went in first. She went deeper inside and saw Violet's orange and black pelt snuggled beside Magenta. Bronze was sitting in a corner, grooming them both.

When he saw Maroon, his eyes widened. "Maroon, you came back!" he exclaimed.

At that moment, Violet and Magenta got up.

Violet looked at Maroon in excitement. "I'm so glad you returned!" she barked.

"Quiet!" Maroon snapped. "There are wolves nearby! We've come to rescue you."

They all looked at each other in pleasure.

They've been stuck in here for days, Maroon thought.

"Let's go!" Mahogany demanded, already making her way outside.

Maroon watched while her friends made their way out the den entrance.

As Magenta, the last one, was crawling out, Maroon heard a voice behind her.

"What are you doing? Guards, don't let them escape!"

Maroon turned and saw the Alpha. Chills crawled down her spine as she realized he must not have gone after Thrash and Slate.

His cold yellow eyes stared into hers, and she could feel her heart pounding so loudly that it brought her back to her senses.

"Run!" she shouted as the two guards realized what was happening and gave chase.

In a full-out run, Maroon could feel the pounding of paws behind her. She could only guess that all her friends were following as they ran to the edge of wolf territory as quickly as they could.

Chapter Twenty-Nine
Slate

Slate felt peaceful. He couldn't feel anything, but he could see the sun as it rose and set. He could see Maroon beside him. He tried to speak to her, but she would vanish, and he would be alone again.

He didn't understand where he was and couldn't feel the pain anymore. He sniffed the flowers at his paws. He liked flowers.

He missed Maroon already. Her beautiful fur, how she cared for him even if she could be mean. He loved her, but he knew she could never accept that, so he had never told her. He had felt that way the whole journey with her, and now he could never be with her.

He was glad he had died instead of her. She didn't deserve it.

He tried to remember how he had died. He had fallen, the wolf's teeth around his neck, sudden pain, and then it had been over. The pain seemed to still be there, though, even in death. He could barely feel the stinging pain. He could also hardly hear Thrash's cries.

"Come fight me!" his friend seemed to say.

Suddenly, he wasn't in the flower field anymore, and the pain was unbearable. He was alive, lying on the ground with the sound of snapping all around him.

He opened his eyes slowly and saw his own blood. It was all around his neck. Then he saw Thrash surrounded by wolves, growling at them.

"You will pay for killing Slate!" Thrash shouted.

Slate thought he should get up and show Thrash that he was not dead, but he couldn't move. He began licking the snow on his face, but it was stained with his own blood.

His tongue lolled, and he looked back at Thrash.

Run! he tried to say. *Don't let them kill you.*

Thrash snarled but seemed to come to his senses as he darted between two wolves. The wolves chased after him.

Slate listened and waited. After a while, he could no longer hear the wolves howling, but he also didn't hear anyone yelp.

Soon, the large group of wolves trudged back, nothing in their jaws. Slate stayed still, and they passed by him.

I hope Maroon and the others got out of wolf territory, he thought. *Those wolves are returning home.*

Slate continued to lie on the ground. Blood stained his caramel-colored fur, making it dark red, while his ear was freezing from the snow underneath. He stifled a whine and waited patiently. He liked being patient.

Finally, he closed his eyes and felt at peace.

***

"Slate!" Thrash's cry rang in his ears.

Slate opened his eyes to see Thrash sitting beside him, hanging his head.

"I should have let you sit out. I didn't know you would be too tired to run for that long," Thrash was saying.

Slate understood. Thrash still thought he was dead.

Smiling, Slate mumbled, "It's okay. I forgive you."

Thrash sprang up. "Slate? You're alive!"

Slate struggled to stand, and Thrash helped him up. Thrash began licking the wounds on his neck. It felt good.

"Is Maroon alive?" Slate rasped, feeling the tingling in his throat from running.

"I hope so," Thrash responded between licks.

When Thrash was done licking the blood away, Slate stood up. His eyes widened as a shock of pain went through him, but he could walk.

Slate yipped in delight and made his way toward wherever Maroon had gone.

***

Maroon ran as fast as she could toward coyote territory. She had to see what had happened.

The guards had tried chasing her and her friends, yet they had all managed to get away. Now Maroon needed to know if Slate was alive.

"You can slow down now!" she heard shouting from behind. "The wolves are gone!"

"No!" Maroon growled and ran on.

Once she saw the rolling hills of coyote territory, she slowed down. She saw Aqua, who was asleep.

Bronze shot past Maroon and ran over to her. Aqua sprang up and dashed over, nuzzling Bronze until he almost stumbled. Her eyes were no longer full of sorrow as they had been for days. Instead, the sorrow was replaced by happiness and relief.

"You made it!" Aqua exclaimed, wagging her tail so hard that Maroon thought it would fall off. Then Aqua looked at Maroon, a big smile on her face, and gave her a nod of thanks.

Maroon felt heart warmed at seeing the two reunited and because she had been able to help make that happen.

She looked around and could see no sign of Slate or Thrash. She froze.

What could have happened to them? she asked herself, worried over the answer.

She decided to stay with Aqua and wait for a little longer. Then she would go search for Slate's body.

Violet came up to her. "You've found your gem!" she announced. "That's great!"

Maroon felt the need to raise her head proudly, but a different feeling overcame her.

"It doesn't matter," she spoke.

"What?" Violet asked. "You've always wanted your own gem. I know how much this means to you."

Maroon shook her head. "Not anymore." She looked Violet in her eyes. "I'm sorry."

Violet widened her eyes in shock. She had never heard Maroon apologize.

"I was so caught up in wanting to be the best. I never listened to you about Slate, and I made a big deal about him. I made it about me, and I wasn't a very good friend," Maroon finished.

Violet smiled and nuzzled her friend.

Maroon felt glad. *This is how it's supposed to be*, she thought. *True friends.*

Then Maroon saw Aqua running up to Violet and Mahogany, all pleased to see each other.

Maroon stood still, listening to the wind and breathing in the warm air. *In a day or two, it will be spring*, she realized.

Sighing, she turned, only to see two distinct shapes approaching from the distance.

"Slate!" she cried, running over to them. "Thrash!"

When she was close enough, she nuzzled Slate, relieved to see him alive.

Slate looked up at her in shock, and then a smile crept across his face, and he wagged his tail slowly.

Thrash stepped in front of Slate and wagged his tail at Maroon.

"Thrash, I'm glad you're okay," she told him, confused as to why Thrash seemed displeased by the fact that Maroon was happier to see Slate.

Slate looked out from behind Thrash, his ears down, feeling a little hurt.

Aqua ran up to stand beside Maroon, happy to see both her friends alive. Then she asked, "Where are my pups?"

Maroon froze. She had been so caught up in the rescue mission and worrying about Slate that she had forgotten all about the pups.

Aqua looked around, concerned. "They aren't still in wolf territory, are they? If they've been in the burrow that long, they may try to escape by themselves."

Maroon felt horror swamp her. How could she have forgotten about the pups?

"Where are they?" Maroon demanded.

Aqua replied, "When the wolves came, I only managed to get them into Magenta's den."

"That's where our distraction was aimed!" Thrash exclaimed.

"They must be terrified!" Slate whined, upset for the pups.

All Maroon could do was stand there in shock. Then, without another word, she turned and bolted straight for Magenta's den, back inside wolf territory.

Chapter Thirty
The Pups

Running at top speed, Maroon could see the trees ahead as they got closer. She would have been able to run even faster if the snow had not been slowing her down.

As she ran, she counted the days in her mind. Winter lasts many, many days. I left before winter. Then I saw the Alpha wolf and his pack hunting moose. After that day, they must have followed my scent back home, which is when they took over. It was already mid-winter when I made it to the trapper's cabin. Then, when Slate and I spent days traveling back home, winter was almost over. So, that means the pups never got fed all winter!

With a gasp, she put on a burst of speed, already inside wolf territory and nearing Magenta's den.

When the maple tree came into sight, she ducked and made her way into the shelter, which was located under the tree.

As soon as she was inside the den, she instinctively threw up on the ground, leaving a pile of regurgitated meat for the pups that might not even still be alive. That was when she saw three small fox pups run straight toward the pile and begin eating.

Maroon let out a sigh of relief. They were alive! However, as she looked at the kits, she could see their skinny bodies revealing their bones, and she noticed how they swallowed the meat as if it were air.

When they finished eating, which had been at a pace so frantic that it surprised Maroon, they sat down in front of her, wagging their tails.

"I'm so hungry!"

"More!"

"We haven't eaten in days!"

They all exclaimed, one after another.

Maroon gave them the last of her food, regurgitating once more to do so.

Once they had finished that, they continued begging for more, and Maroon took a moment to count them.

"Mauve, Taupe, and Teal." she counted, glad to see them all alive.

But it didn't make sense. How could three pups survive most of the winter season without food?

When she asked them, they all fought over who would speak first. Eventually, Mauve said, "Mother told us to get in the den when we heard some scary sounds, so we did. And then we heard Mother getting hurt, so we stayed in the den and waited for the monsters to pass."

Teal butted in, taking over. "Mother would sneak in and feed us as many times as she could, but she said, because of the monsters, she could only feed us once a day, or sometimes we missed a day."

Maroon knew the monsters the pups mentioned were the wolves, but she felt even more awful by Aqua's struggle to keep her kits alive.

Teal went on, "Some days, she managed to bring in a whole squirrel or a bird, but most of the time, we only got to eat her regurgitated food. We are too old to be eating that stuff! Then, some days, she came in to feed us, and we could see new injuries on her. And, usually, on those days, she could not come back the next day."

Maroon felt pity for the pups and for Aqua.

"Why couldn't she sneak you out?" she asked.

It was Taupe who responded. "Because she kept getting caught and attacked by the monsters. She was too weak to carry us, and feeding us all the food in her stomach only made her weaker. She said that if she tried to carry one of us out at a time, she would be too slow to get away. And, if the monsters caught her with one of us, they would have killed her and whoever she was carrying."

Maroon gulped, knowing that if Aqua had carried on starving herself for the kits' sakes, she might not have been able to keep them alive.

"She also said the monsters are speedy, and if we tried to escape on our own, we wouldn't get very far before they killed us," Teal added.

Maroon growled in disgust at how careless the wolves were. Would they really kill an innocent pup as soon as they saw it, simply because it isn't one of their kind?

Maroon remembered the time when she had let the baby rabbit survive and how she still felt pity for something, even if it wasn't a fox.

"Mother hasn't come to feed us for the past couple of days. We think it's because the last time she left, she was attacked by the monsters. It must have been really bad if she left us to starve. But now that you returned, we can leave, right?" Teal asked, wagging his tail.

Maroon nodded. "I'm going to get you out of here, and I want you to know your mother did not abandon you. She is recovering from some injuries but also needs to regain strength. So, I need you to do exactly what I say, understand?"

The pups nodded vigorously. "We understand!"

"Great. Now, who wants to go first?" Maroon asked, looking over at Teal.

He shook his head. "It's okay, but I want my sisters to go first."

Maroon licked Teal's head, appreciating how he wanted his siblings to get to safety. Then she picked up a squirming pup by the scruff. Taking Mauve carefully outside, Maroon was surprised to be greeted by Violet.

Violet was standing by the den, looking around anxiously. When she saw Maroon, she ran over to her.

"Quick, give me the kit, then go and get the others. You won't make it going back and forth between kits before the wolves catch on!" Violet spoke.

Maroon accepted and set Mauve down. She watched as Violet bent her head to pick up the pup then ran off toward coyote territory, where they would be safe.

Turning back to go inside the den, Maroon grabbed Taupe and took her outside. Passing her to the next fox that was waiting—Bronze.

"I'll take my pup from here," he said. "When you go back for Teal, no one else will be waiting for you, so you must get him safely back to coyote territory on your own."

Maroon agreed and made her way back inside the den.

Teal ran up to her, excitement in his eyes. "I am so glad you've returned! It's not as much fun without you." He snuggled up against her.

Maroon nuzzled him. "I missed you. You're growing up so quickly."

"I know! Mother said I'll be a great hunter!" he exclaimed.

"Do you want to know a secret?" Maroon asked.

"Sure," he responded.

"Don't hunt rabbits. They're your friends," she whispered into his ear.

Teal giggled then replied, "I won't. Now can we go? I want to see Mother!"

Maroon grinned. "I'm sure she will be overjoyed to see you." With that, she picked up Teal by the scruff and carried him out of the den.

As soon as the two were out, she began to run back to the others.

Before she got far, she heard a bark from behind. Turning to look, to her horror, she saw the Alpha and his pack. Maroon froze, hearing Teal's gasp of fear from in her jaws.

Maroon faced back toward coyote territory and ran as fast as she could. The snow on the ground dragged against her paws, and it didn't help that she was carrying a heavy pup.

"Get back here!" she heard one of the wolves shout.

The sun was beginning to rise. As the trees thinned and the hills in the distance drew nearer, Maroon almost slowed. She was getting tired; Teal was too heavy. Just a little further, she told herself.

But the wolves continued following her when she burst from the trees and began running on open land.

Why haven't they given up? Maroon thought in terror. They aren't on their territory anymore.

"Don't let this one get away!" a wolf yelled. "Kill them!"

Her teeth ached, and her chest heaved. She couldn't go on like this much longer. Maroon could feel the hot breaths of the wolves against her pelt as they caught up to her.

Though her paws felt like they were on fire, she tried to pick up speed, but the heaviness in her jaw made it almost impossible. Then she looked back one last time.

All the wolves here were chasing her, with the Alpha in the lead. Then she saw Kitsune bolting ahead, right after the Alpha. He seemed almost faster. He ran right up to a rock and leaped off of it. With a screech, he landed on the Alpha's head. Both animals went down in a flurry of snow and claws.

The rest of the pack stopped to see if their Alpha was hurt.

To Maroon's astonishment, Kitsune got up and ran after Maroon, heading back to coyote territory and leaving the wolves to recover from the sudden ambush.

Chapter Thirty-One
Reunited

Maroon set Teal down in the snow and continued walking with him, Kitsune by her side.

"I can't believe you jumped onto the Alpha's head!" Maroon exclaimed, impressed.

Kitsune shrugged. "It was easy. Besides, did you think I was actually going to betray you and join the wolf pack?"

"By the way it turned out, yes! I thought you just now changed your mind and decided to come back to us. Are you saying you were still on our side even after joining the wolves?" Maroon asked.

"I never tell secrets, but making allies gives you the advantage, even if they aren't your true allies, like the wolves," Kitsune answered.

Maroon smirked as she made her way back to the temporary camp.

Aqua jumped up and flew across the ground as soon as they appeared over the rise, racing to get her pup. "Teal! I'm so glad you're alive! I hated leaving you, and I'm so sorry!" she said in delight.

Maroon could see the other pups had also made it to safety, and they happily surrounded Teal.

"Guess who returned?" Maroon announced then watched as everyone's gaze shifted to her.

"Kitsune!" some of them exclaimed while racing over to join him. Thrash was one of them.

When Maroon saw the distrust in most of her friend's eyes, she thought they must still think he actually betrayed them. Therefore, she began to tell them how she had nearly gotten caught by the wolf pack and could have been killed if Kitsune had not saved her. Then she explained that he had joined the wolf pack to create an advantage for the foxes.

After she saw that her friends believed her, she sighed and sat down to rest. Before she could, however, Slate came running up to her with his eyes wide open in fear.

"Do not ever do that to me again!" he wailed, looking her in the eyes.

She stared back, unable to help herself, then said, "You won't have to worry. I'm staying here for now. I won't leave again to go into wolf territory without telling anyone."

Slate looked relieved, and then he pushed a dead vole toward her. "Thrash went hunting when you ran off, so I thought you might want this." He looked down at his paws, and Maroon licked his ears.

"Thank you!" she said then began eating her prey.

Slate got up and started passing around prey to the others. There was enough for everyone, but Thrash refused his food so that he could give it to the pups instead.

As Maroon finished her prey, she saw that all the snow on coyote territory was gone, leaving behind wet grass. She wagged her tail. *I can't wait until the stream runs again without a sheet of ice over it.* She knew that the coyote territory would look like spring before the more shaded sections because there were no trees on the meadows. While hidden beneath the trees, the snow in wolf territory would take longer to melt.

Maroon flattened her ears, annoyed at how she had to call the abandoned forest wolf territory. *Soon, we will get it back*, she told herself.

Just then, she heard a distress call from many of her friends and jumped onto her paws, fur bristling.

"It's a wolf!" they cried. "Coming toward us!"

Maroon looked around to see Aqua standing protectively in front of her pups while the others snarled in anger.

"There's only one!" Bronze yelled. "I think all of us can take it!"

"We do not need more wounds," Thrash growled.

Maroon faced the direction her friends were growling at and indeed saw a wolf. It looked familiar and, as it hobbled forward, she could see it was struggling to make it up the hill.

Only a pup would walk like that, Maroon realized.

"Needle!" she called and raced off toward the pup.

When she reached her, she saw Needle was holding a pinecone.

"Here you go!" Needle exclaimed, setting the pinecone at Maroon's paws.

"What are you doing here?" Maroon growled. "Don't you know it's not safe for a pup like you to be walking around unsupervised?"

Needle flattened her ears. "I know, but ... I ... wanted to see you again, and I brought you a pinecone to apologize for my family chasing you," she said in a sad but quiet voice, making Maroon feel regret for speaking to her in such a harsh tone.

Maroon sighed. "Does your family know you left?"

Needle shook her head. "No, they never do. It's so funny, and when they do notice after I return, they just stare at me without saying anything. It's kind of scary sometimes."

Maroon cocked her head. *Her family is strange. I hope she doesn't end up like them.*

Then Maroon said, "Well, you're safe here, and you can stay if you like."

Needle shook her head, "No, I have to get back soon. But, if your friends live here, I would love to meet them!"

Maroon barked in amusement. Then she picked up her pinecone and led Needle toward the others.

"This is Needle," Maroon said as Needle gazed at the other foxes in awe.

"Hello!" Slate called and came bounding up to them. "My name is Slate. Any friend of Maroon's is a friend of mine, too." He wagged his tail.

"Wow!" Needle exclaimed. "Your fur is almost blue, and you have such a pretty tail. It's tipped black."

"Thank you," Slate replied.

Before Needle could say anything more, Thrash came bounding up and shoved Slate aside.

"Maroon, I think it would be wiser if we just kill the creature. I mean, it's a wolf, and would you really want to agree with Slate? He's too soft," Thrash growled.

Maroon looked over at Slate, who was wincing in pain. Then, in anger, Maroon sprung at Thrash and pushed him away. "Slate's injured!" Maroon yelled, ignoring the shocked look on Thrash's face. "Needle is my friend, and she's just a pup. You only say that because you don't know her like I do! She's very nice and doesn't like how her pack is behaving. Why can't you give her a chance?"

Thrash lashed his tail. "Because her being a pup doesn't make a difference. Her pack will just fill her head with their cruelty. And when she grows up, she'll only know what they told her, and she will be one of them! Remember how you said you were going to use her? Well, now is your chance."

Maroon stared at him then turned when she heard Needle's voice.

"So, you don't trust me? I guess my father was right about foxes. You led me here … to use me." Needle's eyes were filled with hate, but they also held sadness. Then, without a word, she turned and ran.

Maroon glared at Thrash. "Look at what you've done!" Then Maroon raced after Needle.

"Needle, wait up!" Maroon called as she ran. It was not long before she caught up with the slower pup. "Don't listen to him; he doesn't trust anybody. But I know you, and you can trust me."

Needle turned to glare at her. "Then why did you sneak in and free our hostages? That was our only chance to get your friends to leave us alone!"

Maroon was shocked. "You would have saved your friends if they were in danger. I was doing the right thing. You know your pack has done some evil things. You can't side with them, surely?"

145

"I am loyal to my family," Needle began. "I trusted you until I realized that you were using me so that I could go against my family. I'm not stupid. You probably wanted to take me hostage!"

Watching Needle's look of grief and betrayal, Maroon felt pain stabbing her heart. What stung even more was the fact that she was right. Maroon had wanted to use Needle against the wolves. She had never tried to befriend her in the first place.

When Maroon didn't reply, Needle's eyes widened. "You *were* using me!"

"No, Needle, I can explain!" Maroon cried desperately.

"I don't care!" Needle shouted. "You betrayed me! I actually cared about you. No wonder you wanted me so badly. It was all part of your plan!" Needle spoke in grief then raised her head and let out a squeaky pup howl.

In horror, Maroon barked, "What are you doing? You're going to lead your pack over to us!"

Needle eyed her. "So? It doesn't matter what happens to you anymore. I just want to go home." She let out another howl, and Maroon pushed in her to silence her.

But it was too late. She could hear the pack's answering cries in the distance.

Chapter Thirty-Two
Needle's Pack

I care about you!" Maroon cried desperately. "Please, don't do this!"

Needle flattened her ears and, in a sad voice, said, "If you cared so much, why did that big fox say you were planning on using me?"

Maroon growled, remembering Thrash's words, and then she answered, "Because, when I first met you, I did want to use you. But now that my friends are safe and I got to know you better, I don't want anything to happen to you!"

Needle looked unconvinced. "How can I trust you?"

"Because," Maroon began, "you have some good in you. I regret what I originally planned to do with you, but I've made many mistakes, and I'm tired of losing my friends because of them. So, can you trust me, and can we be friends?"

"Maybe ... I mean, you do have pretty fur," Needle said in a more cheerful tone.

Maroon sighed with relief that Needle was acting like her usual self again. But the main problem now was the wolf pack knew where she was, and they were on their way.

"Needle," Maroon spoke desperately, "if you run toward your pack when they arrive, they'll kill me unless you can convince them to leave us alone."

Needle shook her head. "They won't believe me. They hate foxes."

"Then, can you please stay by my side and pretend you've been captured? I know you don't want to be used, but they will attack me the minute I give you back." Maroon told her.

Needle understood. "Of course. I will pretend and tell them not to take a step toward you, or you will hurt me."

"Good," Maroon spoke and stood over Needle, who crouched on the ground, acting sad.

As soon as Maroon saw the wolf pack running toward her, she called out, "Stop! Take another step, and I'll kill this pup!"

All ten wolves stopped in their tracks, Alpha in the lead.

"We heard Needle's cry for help. What's going on?" The Alpha demanded.

"Hand her over, or we'll kill you!" a black wolf shouted, and Maroon guessed it was Shadow, Needle's father.

"If you try to come over and kill me, I'll kill Needle before you even take two steps. You should be wise enough to know how quick and nimble foxes are. You won't stand a chance of getting her back if you try."

The wolves stayed put, fangs showing in frustration.

Maroon looked down at Needle, who winked. *Good.* Maroon thought. *I don't want her to think I'm being serious.*

"How do we get her back?" the Alpha growled, his white pelt glowing.

"I'd like to make a deal," Maroon said, snarling to intimidate the wolves.

Behind her, she could hear the paw steps of her friends coming to stand beside her.

The wolves all growled, a warning not to touch Needle.

Maroon saw Thrash, Bronze, Magenta, Violet, and Slate willing to attack if the wolves got close. *It would be impossible to win*, she thought. *A wolf pack could quickly kill a small group of foxes.*

"Stay back!" Thrash yelled. "Or we won't hesitate to kill the pup."

Maroon nodded, signaling that the wolves already understood what would happen if they came closer. *But, what if they do come closer?* Maroon thought as she worried. *Will I have to kill Needle like I said I would? I wouldn't really kill her. Instead, I would run away. But, what if one of my friends killed her without realizing I was pretending?* She dug her claws into the grass in fear.

"I'd like to make a deal," Maroon repeated. "Then you can get your pup back."

Her friends all nodded in agreement and stared down at the wolves.

"What sort of deal?" the Alpha growled.

"I'll give you Needle if, in return, you give us back our forest," Maroon said in satisfaction.

Behind her, she could hear barks of agreement from her friends while the wolves growled in rage.

"We worked hard for that spot!" a gray wolf spoke. "We can't let them have it."

"It was theirs first, but we did rightfully claim it," another wolf said.

"We should just kill them all right now. Even if they do kill Needle, at least we can get revenge."

All the wolves spoke as one, pelts bristling in anger. They didn't want to lose the territory they had worked so hard for, even if it meant holding hostages and attacking everyone they saw.

Then a tan wolf padded up to stand beside the Alpha. Maroon remembered him as Steel and how many encounters she'd had with him.

"We can't lose another one, can we?" Steel spoke to the Alpha. "I mean, not after what happened at the trapper's cabin."

All the wolves bowed their heads in grief, and Maroon realized what might have occurred at the trapper's cabin.

"Did someone die?" she asked, forgetting she was talking to wolves.

She heard a whine from Needle and looked down to see her usually cheerful face was overtaken by sadness.

"We will not tell you!" the Alpha growled, his yellow eyes blazing.

"Spruce," Steel began, ignoring his Alpha's protests. "We moved into that territory, thinking it was safe. We didn't know the consequences."

"Silence!" the Alpha shouted.

Steel went on, "We settled in and made ourselves at home, but Spruce … he was just a pup."

"Enough!" the Alpha shouted again.

"He was so young. The whole pack was walking near the trapper's cabin." Steel paused to take a breath.

The Alpha had stopped his shouting and instead growled as Steel told the story.

"We were all passing through. We didn't know someone lived in that trapper's house. When Spruce and I were lagging behind. Someone suddenly emerged from the cabin and pointed something at Spruce. I tried to save him, but it was too late. There was a bang, and Spruce fell … I knew he was dead. Before I could even do anything else, the trapper pointed the stick at us, and we had to run. Kitsune helped us out. But Spruce … he was Needle's brother."

Maroon gasped and looked at Needle, who gazed back expressionlessly.

No wonder Needle was the only pup, she realized. *I would have never known.*

"You think foxes care about a wolf pup?" The Alpha laughed. "Just look at them. They're heartless."

"Not all of them," Steel replied, looking at Maroon. "Some care, like Kitsune. Maybe they aren't heartless. They did risk their lives to get their family back."

"Well, they don't care about anyone but their own species. Why do you think Kitsune helped them? He was lying when he joined us. These foxes will kill Needle, whatever it takes." The Alpha snickered.

"And because of that, I think we should move," Steel snapped. "They will not settle until they've gotten back their territory, so we should just look for another forest."

The Alpha glared deep into Maroon's eyes, and she felt a strange sense to submit, but she remained strong and glared back. The Alpha seemed shocked by this boldness.

Maroon looked around. All her friends, including Thrash, were averting their gazes and crouching in fear. Maroon was the only one standing tall.

Are the Alpha's eyes so frightening that not even Thrash can do anything? she thought.

Then, full of anger at the wolves who stole her home, hurt her friends, and tried to kill her, Maroon revealed her fangs and locked eyes with the Alpha.

"I'm tired of running away," she spoke as she took a step forward. "I'm tired of being afraid. I won't look away when something scares me. You do not scare me!"

The white Alpha wolf widened his eyes. "There's something wrong with that fox!"

With that, the other wolves began to back away and leave.

"Come back! They're just foxes!" the Alpha called out to his fleeing pack. Then, in anger when they didn't respond, the Alpha swung around and ran after them, leading them beyond the stolen territory.

Once the wolves were tiny dots on the horizon, Maroon looked at Needle, who smiled at her.

"Good job," she said then bounded after her pack.

Maroon stood with her friends as they watched Needle disappear into the distance.

Chapter Thirty-Three
Maroon

Maroon crouched low, creeping closer to a finch. It was between two trees, pecking at the grass.

"I've caught a vole already," she said quietly. "Thrash also went out hunting, so if he brings back some prey, we should have enough for almost everyone."

The finch lifted its head, looking around with its beady eyes. When no other sound seemed to disturb the bird, it began poking at its feathers in a grooming session.

Maroon took the chance and leaped. The finch tweeted in alarm and spread its wings.

Maroon crashed onto the ground, and dirt showered into her eyes and mouth. She let out a yelp of shock. Then, looking up in the nick of time, she saw the finch disappear through the branches. It had gotten away. Maroon let out a bark of anger, thrashing her tail in rage. Then she calmed down.

It's just doing what it needs to do to survive. Just like I am when I hunt, Maroon told herself, though she was still upset about losing her prey.

Shaking all the dirt from her pelt, she picked up the vole she had caught earlier and began walking back to the camp.

After Needle had pretended to have been kidnapped and the wolves had left the forest, Maroon and her friends had returned to their territory while the wolves moved elsewhere. Maroon hoped the new wolf territory was not located somewhere nearby. She didn't want any more problems with them.

As she drew closer to the main area where all her friends were staying, she heard a sound. The chirp of a bird.

Maroon instinctively crouched down, listening for the bird. When she heard it again, she turned toward the sound, stalking her prey.

By now, she could see it was a robin struggling to pull a worm out of the ground. Maroon waited for the right moment, and then she pounced, landing on the bird. *Yes!* she thought. *Finally, I can bring back enough prey for everyone. Hopefully, Thrash got something, too.*

As she picked up the robin and vole, she breathed in the fresh spring air.

I missed my home, she thought. *Now I can get back to my log.*

Soon enough, she reached the open clearing where she saw Aqua resting in a flower patch with Bronze by her side. Her wounds were almost healed, and they sat together watching their pups play. Violet was talking to Magenta, sharing news. Mahogany was busy adding more items to her collection, such as pinecones, sticks, and moss. Slate and Thrash seemed to be discussing something, but their ears were flat, as if they didn't like what they were talking about. Maroon saw Kitsune say something to the pups as they played.

When she padded up to the open clearing, Slate broke away from Thrash, seeming relieved, and bounded up to her.

"You brought back prey! Set it over here. Thrash returned before you, but we should have enough to feed everyone," Slate said, welcoming her.

Maroon set both the vole and the robin on the prey that Thrash had brought back. He had killed a squirrel, some birds, and another vole. *He caught enough for everyone,* she thought.

"Maroon has returned!" Teal exclaimed. "Can we eat now?"

"Sure," Aqua spoke.

With that, all her friends began eating and sharing the prey that they had collected.

***

"What does she look like?" Teal asked, begging Maroon to tell him.

"She was a mix of gray and white, with a black paw and blue eyes," Maroon said. "Needle was my friend."

"And she was a wolf?" Teal asked again. "Was she a nice wolf?"

Maroon replied, "She was a wolf pup. She was very nice, but her pack might raise her to become one of them, so it's not worth looking for her anymore."

Teal had not known about Needle until he pleaded for Maroon to tell him about everything that had happened with the wolves and how she had rescued everyone.

"Would you?" Teal asked, and it took Maroon a moment to realize he meant look for Needle.

Maroon thought then shook her head. "Needle is with her pack now. They won't bother us anymore."

"But you could visit her," Teal responded. "I bet she misses you. I missed you when you left." Then he got up and bounded over to Aqua.

Maroon sat, thinking about what Teal had said. Maybe someday she could go looking for Needle. Maroon thought, *If she would even want to see me after I forced her family to move.*

Then, deciding that today wasn't the right time to think about that, she got up and started toward Violet's den. The sun shined brightly, melting any snow that had survived this long into spring.

She looked down at her gem as she made it to the small boulders that Violet lived under. The purple rock sparkled in the light. Maroon smiled. She couldn't get rid of her gem. It reminded her of her friends, and Violet was her best friend.

Maroon made her way toward the burrow's entrance, looking forward to talking with Violet. But when she approached the boulders, she felt an unsettling feeling and thoughts of the wolf pack poured into her mind.

"Just where do you think you are going, fox?"

"Guards, don't let them escape!"

"The wolves did this."

"There's something wrong with that fox!"

The thoughts all exploded in her head. The memories were too much.

She dug her claws into the ground and flattened her ears.

"Stop it!" she cried when the thoughts wouldn't go away.

"Maroon?" she heard someone bark from behind.

She turned and saw Slate padding up to her.

"Are you okay?"

She looked at him, his face full of worry.

"I'm fine," she snapped. "Just a daydream."

"Was it a frightening daydream?" he asked, cocking his head.

Maroon realized that she could trust him.

"Yes," she replied. "I was thinking about the wolves; that's all."

"If it makes you feel better, I think you are brave. You would not let any wolf touch you. I was unlucky when they caught me, but you would do anything to protect your friends," Slate told her.

After hearing Slate's words, she nuzzled him, pushing the thoughts of the wolf pack behind her.

"You make me feel better," she whispered.

Slate pulled back with his ears flat. "I am not supposed to," he said quietly, staring at the ground. "I will see you later." He sprang up and ran away.

Maroon stared after him, confused. *What happened to him*, she thought. *I thought we were friends. So, why is he acting strange all of a sudden?*

She got up and slowly walked toward her log, a sinking feeling in her heart.

"I like him more than a friend," Maroon told herself. "I think he does, too. But what's happened to him?"

***

Waking up with a yawn, Maroon stretched. It was night, and the moon was up. Magenta had agreed with everyone's desire for her to host another one of her gatherings since it had been a while since they last had one.

Maroon easily slid through the bramble bushes surrounding her log, making her way toward the open clearing where the gatherings were usually held.

Approaching the clearing, she saw Teal and his siblings chasing each other.

Thrash was talking with Slate again, and he didn't seem too happy. Aqua and Bronze were sharing prey. Violet was talking with both Mahogany and Magenta. Kitsune was also there, though he was dozing in the ferns, or maybe he was just pretending.

As Maroon approached, she saw Violet inviting her into the group by flicking her tail. Maroon sat beside Violet, listening to the conversation.

"Hopefully, they don't come back," Mahogany said, and Maroon quickly realized they were talking about the wolves.

"If they do, I'm sure Maroon or Thrash could help drive them away again," Violet replied. "They both helped."

Maroon grinned, happy to be the one accepting the praise.

"I bet, if they ever come back, Maroon could easily kill that pup," Magenta said. "If we kill the last of their pups, they will think twice before trying to claim our territory."

Maroon shifted, uncomfortable with what she had just heard. Should she tell them that she had befriended Needle? What would they think of her then?

Violet seemed to notice Maroon's unease. "Mahogany, Magenta, why don't you both start the feast?"

They both nodded and padded away.

"What's wrong?" Violet asked. "Was it something they said?"

Maroon shrugged. "I guess I don't like it when someone talks about killing Needle!"

"Is Needle that wolf pup?" Violet guessed. "Well, she would kill a couple of fox kits if she got the chance. Besides, she's a wolf and will grow up just like her evil pack."

Maroon grumbled. *Why does everyone keep saying that Needle will become evil just like her pack? Surely, she will notice her family isn't a good pack, and she will leave, won't she?* Maroon thought, hoping her friends weren't right about Needle becoming like the other wolves.

"The feast is about to begin," Violet interrupted her thoughts. "Why don't you come?"

Maroon nodded and followed Violet to a prey pile stocked full of delicious food. Voles, mice, birds, berries, and fruit lay before them. There were also acorns and mushrooms.

"This feast," Magenta announced to everyone as they crowded around the pile, "is to celebrate getting our territory back!"

Everyone either cheered in joy or nodded in agreement.

"With that," Magenta continued, "help yourselves."

All the foxes began picking out prey. Maroon noticed how many of her friends left the best food for someone else. Deciding to do the same, Maroon took a bird, leaving the juicer prey for another lucky fox.

As she ate, Slate nosed a mouse over to her.

"I already have something," Maroon spoke with her mouth full.

"I know, but it is a feast." Then, in a quieter tone, he added, "I caught this just for you." Then he slunk away and sat between Violet and Bronze, looking around nervously.

What's gotten into him? she thought. *When we journeyed together, we got along. Well, sort of ... Is someone here bothering him?*

As the feast continued, Maroon finished her bird and started on the mouse. Listening to everyone talking as they ate, she observed how they mostly talked about how good it was to be home.

After some time, Aqua and Bronze left early. All three of their pups had fallen asleep, so they returned to their den for the night.

Maroon was finishing up some berries, feeling stuffed from eating the feast. All of her other friends felt the same. Although they had gathered a lot of food, the foxes didn't waste any of it, especially the meat.

As soon as Kitsune was done, he left to sleep in his tiny burrow, which had recently been dug for him. Kitsune had wanted to stay at the trapper's cabin during the winter then travel again to find a desert area, yet he had agreed to stay here for the rest of his life instead.

Thrash had also agreed to stay and moved out of coyote territory to make a den in the forest.

"I'm ready to sleep now," Maroon said to the remaining friends, who would also leave for their own dens soon. "I'll see you all tomorrow."

"Goodnight, Maroon," Violet called. "Thank you for being my friend."

***

Maroon stirred in her nest. She hadn't gotten a minute of sleep and was growling in irritation. She was so sleepy, but no dreams came to her. Instead, she was distracted by what Slate had said and how he had acted. *Maybe something is bothering him.* Thinking, she sat upright. *Perhaps I could figure out what it could be.*

Shaking out her fur, she emerged from her log. Breathing in the night air, she made her way to the stream. She wanted a drink before she went anywhere.

Feeling the sweet tang of water touch her tongue, she drank until she was full. Then she sat up and stared at a blade of grass, thinking intently.

"Maroon?" she heard a soft voice speak quietly.

Maroon jumped, startled, but then she turned to see Slate, who was sitting on a small hill, looking at her.

"Slate? What are you doing here?" Maroon spoke as she approached him.

"I could not sleep, so I came to look at the view," he replied.

Maroon walked over and sat next to him. She watched him until he flicked his ear. Then she asked, "Is something bothering you?"

He looked at his paws. "No, not really."

Maroon licked his nose, which she had never done before, but it seemed to cheer him up.

"It is just Thrash," Slate told her. "He doesn't really like me."

"Is he mean to you?" Maroon asked in surprise.

Slate shook his head. "He tells me I should stop hanging around you and wants you to be around him more."

Maroon cocked her head, upset with Thrash. *Why won't he let me be with Slate? Is he jealous?*

"Don't listen to him," she said. "I like you, anyway."

Slate smiled and nuzzled her.

Maroon wrapped her tail around his, and they both looked into each other's eyes for a moment. The crickets chirped, and the moon shed light down on the two.

This feels right, she thought. *I'm finally home.*

With that, Maroon turned her head to look up at the stars with an old enemy by her side.

The End!

About the Author

Grace Tasker lives in Colorado with her family, pet dog, and a bearded dragon. She loves all animals and has a passion for art, writing, animation, and learning ASL. She has a witty, fun-loving, and imaginative nature. She is involved in tech theater and loves designing props for musicals and plays.

Her interest in psychology helps her write characters in a fascinating and realistic way.

Made in the USA
Middletown, DE
30 October 2023

41529291R10102